E. L. DOCTOROW
ANDREW'S BRAIN

ABACUS

ABACUS

First published in Great Britain in 2014 by Little, Brown

A CIP catalogue record for this book
is available from the British Library.

ISBN 978-1-4087-0498-1

Printed and bound in Great Britain by
Clays Ltd, St Ives plc

Papers used by Abacus are from well-managed forests
and other responsible sources.

MIX
Paper from
responsible sources
FSC® C104740

Abacus
An imprint of
Little, Brown Book Group
100 Victoria Embankment
London EC4Y 0DY

An Hachette UK Company
www.hachette.co.uk

www.littlebrown.co.uk

ANDREW'S BRAIN

BY E. L. DOCTOROW

To

M.

I

I CAN TELL YOU about my friend Andrew, the cognitive scientist. But it's not pretty. One evening he appeared with an infant in his arms at the door of his ex-wife, Martha. Because Briony, his lovely young wife after Martha, had died.

Of what?

We'll get to that. I can't do this alone, Andrew said, as Martha stared at him from the open doorway. It happened to have been snowing that night, and Martha was transfixed by the soft creature-like snowflakes alighting on Andrew's NY Yankees hat brim. Martha was like that, enrapt by the peripheral things as if setting them to music. Even in ordinary times, she was slow to respond, looking at you with her large dark rolling protuberant eyes. Then the smile would come, or the nod, or the shake of the head. Meanwhile the heat from her home drifted through the open door and fogged up Andrew's eyeglasses. He stood there behind his foggy lenses like a blind man in the snowfall and was without volition when at last she reached out, gently took the swaddled infant from him, stepped back, and closed the door in his face.

This was where?

Martha lived then in New Rochelle, a suburb of New York, in a neighborhood of large homes of different styles—Tudor, Dutch Colonial, Greek Revival—most of them built in the 1920s and '30s, houses set back from the street with tall old Norway maples the predominant trees. Andrew ran to his car and came back with a baby carrier, a valise, two plastic bags filled with baby needs. He banged on the door: Martha, Martha! She is six months old, she has a name, she has a birth certificate. I have it here, open the door please, Martha, I am not abandoning my daughter, I just need some help, I need help!

The door opened and Martha's husband, a large man, stood there. Put those things down, Andrew, he said. Andrew did as he was told and Martha's large husband thrust the baby back into his arms. You've always been a fuck-up, Martha's large husband said. I'm sorry your young wife has died but I expect that she's dead of some stupid mistake on your part, some untimely negligence, one of your thought experiments, or famous intellectual distractions, but in any event something to remind us all of that gift you have of leaving disaster in your wake.

Andrew put the baby in the baby carrier that lay on the ground, lifted the carrier with the baby, and walked slowly back to his car, nearly losing his balance on the slick path. He fastened a seat belt around the carrier in the backseat, returned to the house, picked up the plastic bags and the valise and carried them to the car. When everything was secured, he closed the car door, drew himself up, turned, and found Martha standing there with a shawl around her shoulders. All right, she said.

[*thinking*]

Go on. . . .

No, I'm just thinking of something I read about the pathogenesis of schizophrenia and bipolar disease. The brain biologists are going to get to that with their gene sequencing, finding the variations in the genome—those protein suckers attached to the teleology. They'll give them numbers and letters, snipping away a letter here, adding a number there, and behold the disease will be no more. So, Doc, you're in trouble with your talking cure.

Don't be too sure.

Trust me, you'll be on unemployment. What else can we do as eaters of the fruit of the tree of knowledge but biologize ourselves? Expunge the pain, extend the life. You want another eye, say, in the back of your head? That can be arranged. Put your rectum in your knee? Not a problem. Even give you wings if you want, though the result would not be flying aloft but more like giant skips, floating megastrides as on those tracks that are like flattened escalators moving along the long airport corridors. And how do we know God would not want this, perfecting his fucked-up imperfect idea of life as an irremediable condition? We're his backup plan, his fail-safe. God works through Darwin.

So Martha took the baby after all?

I think also of how we decay in our rotting coffins, and how we reincarnate, the little microgenetic fragments of us sucked into the gut of a blind worm that rises it knows not why to wiggle in the rain-soaked soil only to die on the sharp beak of a house wren. Hey, that's my living genome-fragged ID shat from the sky and landing with a plop on the branch of a tree and dripping over the branch like a wet bandage. And lo! I am become a nutrient of a tree fighting for its life. That's true, you know, how those immobile standing-fast vascular creatures silently struggle for their existence as do we with one another, trees fighting for the same sun, the same soil in which they root themselves, and strewing the seeds that will become their forest enemies, like the princes to their king fathers in the ancient empires. But they're not completely motionless. In a high wind they do their dance of despair, the trees in heavy leaf swaying this way and that, throwing their arms up in their helpless fury of being what they are. . . . Well, it's a short step from anthropomorphism to hearing voices.

You hear voices?

Ah, I knew that would get your attention. Usually as I'm falling asleep. In fact I know I'm falling asleep when I hear them. And that wakes me up. I didn't want to tell you this and here I am telling you.

What do they say?

I don't know. Weird things. But I don't really hear them. I mean, they are definitely voices but at the same time they're soundless.

Soundless voices.

Yes. It's as if I hear the meanings of the words that are spoken without the sound. I hear the meanings but I know they are words that are spoken. Usually by different people.

Who are these people?

I don't know any of them. One girl asked me to sleep with her.

Well, that's normal—a man would dream that.

It's more than a dream. And I didn't know her. A girl in a long summer frock down to her ankles. And she wore running shoes. She had delicate freckles under her eyes, and her face seemed pale with sunlight even as she stood in the shade. Pretty enough to break your heart! She took my hand.

Well, that's more than a voice, certainly more than a soundless voice.

7

I think what happens is that I hear the meaning and provide an illustration in my mind. . . .

So, might we get back to Andrew the cognitive scientist?

I find myself reluctant to tell you that I hear the soundless voices too when I'm up and about in my daily life. But why shouldn't I? There was a morning on my way to work, for instance, when I had picked up my coffee and newspaper from the deli and was waiting at a stoplight. Watching the red seconds run down. And a voice said: *As long as you're standing there, why don't you fix the screen door.* It was so real, so close to an actual sounded voice, that I turned around to see who was in back of me. But there was no one, I was alone on that corner.

And what was the illustration you provided when you heard that remark?

It was an older woman. I put myself in her kitchen doorway. It was some sort of broken-down farm. I thought it might be in western Pennsylvania. There was an old flatbed truck in the yard. The woman wore a faded housedress. She looked up from the sink, totally unsurprised, and said that. At the kitchen table a small girl was drawing with a crayon. Was she the woman's granddaughter? I didn't know. She looked at me and turned back to her drawing and suddenly violently scribbled all over it with her crayon—whatever she had drawn she was now destroying.

Are you in fact the man you call your friend Andrew, the cognitive scientist who brought an infant child to the home of his ex-wife?

Yes.

And are you telling me that you dreamt you ran away and found yourself standing at the screen door of some broken-down farmhouse somewhere?

Well, it was not a dream, it was a voice. Try to pay attention. This voice brought back to me how it was when I needed to get away after my baby with Martha had died and my life with Martha with it. I didn't care where I went. I got on the first bus I saw at the Port Authority. I fell asleep on the bus, and when I woke it was winding its way through the hills of western Pennsylvania. We stopped at a small travel agency in one of these towns and I got off to walk around the town square. It was two or three in the morning, everything was closed of what there was, a drugstore, a five-and-ten, a picture framer, a movie theater, and taking up all one side of the square a sort of Romanesque courthouse. In the square of dead brown grass was a greenish-black Civil War statue of a man on a horse. By the time I got back to the travel agency, the bus was gone. So I walked out of town, over the railroad tracks, past some warehouses, and

9

about a mile or two away—it was dawn now—I came upon this broken-down scrabbly-looking farm. I was hungry. I walked into the yard. No sign of life there so I walked around to the back of the house and found my-self standing at a screen door. And there were these two just as I'd made them up or thought I had, the child and the old woman. And the old woman was the one who'd made that remark the morning I stood with my coffee and paper in Washington, D.C., waiting for the light to change.

So what you're saying is that you ran away and found yourself at the actual screen door of some broken-down farmhouse somewhere in Pennsylvania that you'd previ-ously imagined?

No, dammit. That's not what I'm claiming. I did get on that bus and the trip was exactly as I've said. The shabby little town, the dirt farm. And when I got to the house it's true that those two people were in the kitchen, the old woman and the child with her crayons. There was also a roll of flypaper hanging under the ceiling light, and it was black with flies sticking to it. So it was all very real. But nobody asked me to fix the screen door.

No?

I'm the one who suggested that I fix it. I was tired and hungry. I didn't see a man anywhere. I thought if I of-fered some sort of handyman's help, they'd let me wash up, give me something to eat. I didn't want charity. So I smiled and said: Good morning. I'm a bit lost, but I see your screen door needs mending and I think I can fix it if you will offer me a cup of coffee. I'd noticed the door couldn't close properly, the upper hinge had pulled away from the frame, the mesh was slack. As a screen door it was quite useless, which is why they had hung flypaper from the ceiling light cord. So you see, it was not a pre-ternatural vision that drew me to that place. I had taken that bus ride and seen that farm and those two people and then blanked them out of my mind until the morn-ing in Washington when I was standing on the corner waiting for the red seconds to wind down and heard—

You were then working in Washington?

—yes, as a government consultant, though I can't tell you doing what—and heard the voice of the old woman saying more or less what I had said when I appeared out-side her screen door. Except in her voice the words had a judgmental tone—as if I had given her an insight into my hapless existence, to the effect of: "As long as you're standing there why don't you for once make yourself use-ful and fix the screen door." There's a term for this kind of experience in your manual, is there not?

Yes. But I'm not sure we're talking about the same kind of experience.

We have our manual too, you know. Your field is the

mind, mine is the brain. Will the twain ever meet? What's important about that bus trip is that I had reached the point where I felt anything I did would bring harm to anyone I loved. Can you know what that's like, Mr. Analyst sitting in his ergonomic chair? I couldn't know in advance how to avoid disaster, as if no matter what I did something terrible would follow. So I got on that bus, just to get away, I didn't care. I wanted to tamp down my life, devote myself to mindless daily minutiae. Not that I had succeeded. What he said made that clear.

What who said?

Martha's large husband.

When Andrew stepped inside the front door he saw Martha's large husband putting on his coat and hat and Martha walking up the stairs with the baby in her arms while turning back the little hood, unzipping the snowsuit. Andrew took note of a large well-appointed house, much grander than the house he and Martha had lived in as man and wife. The entrance hall had a dark parquet floor. Out of the corner of his eye he saw to his left a comfortable living room with stuffed furniture, and a fireplace with a fire going, and on the wall over the mantel the portrait of what he took to be some Russian czar in a long robe with an Orthodox cross on a chain and a crown that looked like an embroidered cap. To the right was a book-lined study with Martha's black Steinway. The staircase, carpeted in dark red with brass rods at the bottoms of the risers, was elegantly curved with a mahogany banister that Martha was not holding as she mounted the stairs with the baby in her arms. Martha wore slacks. Andrew noticed that she had maintained her figure and he found himself considering, as he hadn't for many years, the shape and tensile strength of her behind. The coat of Martha's large husband was of the round-shouldered style with a caped collar and sleeves that flared out. Nobody wore coats like that anymore. The hat, a sporty crushproof number, was too small for Martha's large husband's head.

Martha said without turning her head: Go with him, Andrew, in the same quiet commanding tone of voice she used when they were married.

Andrew ran ahead and opened the passenger's car door. He was grateful when Martha's large husband maneuvered himself into the seat. Off they went to Martha's large husband's preferred pub. He directed Andrew wordlessly, pointing left or right at the intersections, grunting and pointing to the parking space when they'd arrived. It was a bar in a mall. Andrew anticipated a conversation, some sort of understanding—they after all had the shared experience of the same wife—but once they were seated at the bar with their drinks in front of them in tall crystal-cut glasses, and though Andrew waited for the conversation to begin, Martha's large husband did not speak. So Andrew said something along these lines:

Everything you believe about me is true. It is true I accidentally killed my baby girl that I had with Martha: In good faith I fed her the medicine I believed had been prescribed by our pediatrician. The druggist sent over the wrong medicine and I was not as alert as I should have been, I'd done a day on my dissertation in cognitive science, I had spent hours at the lab, plus department meetings and so forth, and I dutifully fed the medicine into her tiny mouth with an eyedropper. All night I did this every two hours, until the child stopped crying and was dead. I didn't know it was dead, I thought it had finally gone to sleep. I was tired and lay down myself, it had been my task to stay up with a sick child because Martha was exhausted—she'd been teaching her master class in piano all day, and I was the man, after all. What woke me was Martha screaming, it was not human, it was the sound of a huge forest animal with its leg caught in a steel trap, and maybe not even an animal of the present time, but something like its paleontological version.

Martha's large husband said, looking into the blue mirror behind the bar: When an animal's leg is caught in a trap, do you know what it does to free itself? It chews the leg off. But of course it is forever disabled and unable to reasonably provide for itself and live a normal life.

You mean Martha, Andrew said.

Yes. And so I have been permanently crippled as well, having in love married an irremediably damaged woman who can no longer practice her profession. Thanks to Sir Andrew the Pretender.

Is that who I am, Sir Andrew the Pretender?

Yes, whose well-meaning, gentle, kindly disposed, charming ineptitude is the modus operandi of the deadliest of killers. Let's have another.

When Andrew picked up his glass to down his drink quickly so that he could honor his moral debt to Martha's large husband by having another, which he didn't really want, the glass slipped from his hand. In his attempt to grab it, Andrew hooked the bowl of peanuts off the bar with the edge of his jacket sleeve, and flustered by the sudden obligation to right two things simultaneously he lost them both, the glass and its contents, including its ice cubes and wedge of lime, following the cascade of peanuts onto Martha's large husband's lap.

Were you offended by what he said—Martha's large husband? Did that anger you?

No, he's an opera singer. Opera is the art of unconstrained emotions. Something happens and they sing about it for hours. What he said, though expressed in a bass-baritone voice of great and intimidating czarist resonance, was true. I could not be offended or made angry, not only because I already knew that about myself, but because there is a caesura in my brain—so that honor, among other virtues, is nothing I connect to. I have none. Deep down, at the bottom of my soul, if such exists, I am finally unmoved by what I've done. A faint tinge of regret for dead babies, for dead wives, for the fires I've inadvertently started, and all such disasters can make me run in my dreams to someplace where I can't do any harm, but in this waking life I am numb to my guilt.

But after that terrible event of the baby's death you did get onto a bus to western Pennsylvania. Didn't you? Or are you saying now you dreamt the whole thing?

No, what actually happened is the way I've described it.

Well, then, in your waking life as in your dreams, weren't you running away? That doesn't sound like someone numb to his guilt.

You can have such moments but they're not characteristic, they're incidental to the predominant state of mind. Remnants of whatever humanity I may have once had.

I see.

Because the truth is, I just shrug and soldier on. As kind as I am, as well-meaning and helpful as I try to be, I have no feelings finally, for good or ill. In the depths of my being, no matter what happens, I am left cold, impenetrable to remorse, to grief, to happiness, though I can pretend well enough even to the point of fooling myself. I am trying to say I am finally, terribly, unfeeling. My soul resides in a still, deep, beautiful, emotionless, calm cold pond of silence. But I am not fooled. A killer is what I am. And to top things off I am incapable of punishing myself, taking my own life in despair of the wreck I've made of people's lives, helpless infants or women I love. And that's what Martha's large husband the opera singer failed to understand when he condemned me, perhaps in the hope that I would see the light and off myself. [*thinking*] Of course I would never do that.

So now Martha had a baby after all, a replacement for her lost child.

I hadn't thought of it that way. I didn't mean to give her the baby outright. I just needed some help. For a year or two. I was still in shock from Briony's death. But Martha took possession of the kid as if she was the rightful parent.

Did that bother you?

I was in no position to argue. Do I have to spell it

out? Are you that dense? I'd killed one baby. Did you want me to kill another? Anyway, I'll reconnect some-day. She has Briony's pale blue eyes. The same fair coloring.

Was Martha's large husband correct that you bore a responsibility for your wife's death?

Not entirely.

What does that mean?

It was indirect—not directly causal.

So what happened? You mean in childbirth?

No, I do not mean that.

How did she die?

I don't want to talk about it. [*thinking*] I can tell you that after killing his baby with Martha, Andrew took a low-paying adjunct professorship at a small state college out west that he'd never heard of.

Why?

Why do you think? Because it was far away. Because after she divorced him Martha liked to be seen standing outside his apartment building when he came home from work. She would take a drag on her cigarette, drop it on the ground, step on it, and walk away.

So in her eyes only you were to blame—you and only you.

Who else?

What about the pharmacist? Did you think of suing?

Oh, God, you have no idea, do you, of the obliteration of social reality in the aftermath of something like this. The brain all lit up with the realization that what you did is unchangeable. To sue someone? Was there redemption in that? What would you gain—money? Jesus, I don't know why I talk to you. Would suing someone bring the infant back? And whom should we have sued? The pediatrician who phoned in the prescription? the druggist who filled it? the delivery boy who brought it? Where had the thing gone wrong? Whom should we have sued? I could have read the label. I could have sued myself. I had administered the medicine. That's all Martha could see, that I had done the thing, finally, I and no one else.

And you agreed with her.

I did. It was me, all over.

And now here was Andrew, self-exiled to this state college in the foothills of a mountain range called the Wasatch. At first I liked the mountains. I got there early in September, a still-warm summer's end with traces of the old winter's snow on the mountaintops. That gave me a sense of the nonhuman world we live in. You get that when you're out of the city. Americans like to catch rides in that world.

What is this you're saying?

Skiing down a mountain—that's one of the free rides. Sea combers, white-water rivers. A wind to hang in. Free rides of the planet. They're all there for you to get on or get off or get killed.

I see. So it turned out to be a good change of scenery for you.

Not really. I don't suppose you've ever lived under a mountain. Wasatches ruled that town. After a day or two the truth dawned on me. You got up in the morning, they were there. You pulled into a gas station, and they were there. They were there in their stolid immensity, and that was that. You were colonized. They negotiated the light, they had to pass on it before it got to you.

I don't understand.

They took in the light, they'd bounce it down or suck it up as was their wont. It was a kind of mountain bureaucracy, and nobody could do anything about it, least of all the sun. The college had a deal for visiting faculty with a local suite motel. Formica countertop kitchenette. Laminated furniture. And turquoise-and-rust curtains to suggest the Native American heritage. That was also what the mountains did—invite a corporate culture. I was the college's halfhearted attempt to expand its offerings. I was the one-man Department of Brain Science. I had no one to talk to. My colleagues, if that's what they were in their polite and distant way, were bores. I was lonely and miserable.

One day, as Andrew walked past the college gymnasium, a building much like an airplane hangar, he saw through the open doors a population of gymnasts and track and fielders: broad jumpers, high jumpers, hurdlers, shot putters, pole vaulters, pommel horsers, steel ringers, balance beamers, trampoliners. The intensity, the concentration of each of them on what they were doing, everyone moving in a differentiated self-absorbed effort while ignoring everyone else, put him in mind of a culture of squiggling DNA molecules, so that if he waited long enough all these jumping and vaulting and circling squiggles would assemble themselves into the double helix of a genetic code. He was particularly attracted to one of the gymnasts working out on the high bar, a blond girl swinging to and fro in what could have been a one-piece swimsuit. She seemed more human than the rest of them, as if she were actually reveling in the exercise. But this swinging maneuver was preparatory—once she had the velocity, up she rose to a handstand, holding herself upside down and straight as an arrow, only to lazily begin to fall backward into another sequence of three-hundred-and-sixty-degree suspensefully-pausing-at-the-top rotations. And then to fall into another spin, but forward this time, like a clock hand gone crazy. Andrew, not wanting to be seen staring, quickly walked on when she completed her routine with a final spin around and a leap through the air with a perfect landing in a half crouch, arms outstretched.

Which reminds me, once I saw a woman do a complete somersault in the air, launching herself into an in-flight three-hundred-and-sixty-degree head-over-heels maneuver before landing nimbly on her bare feet. You'd think that was impossible.

Where was this?

She leapt into the air not from any platform but from the floor of what I took to be some sort of dance studio, and then grabbed her ankles and curled into her remarkable airborne spin. She wore a man's ribbed sleeveless undershirt and a pleated billowing pair of bloomers and did not look at me for approval once the maneuver was completed. A short plain dark-haired little woman but with good round calves and slim feet that widened at the metatarsals. But the man, her putative manager, a big bulky fellow who had gotten me to come see this, said, What do you think? And I had to tell him the act needed beefing up. Her trick had taken only a few seconds.

That's not enough for an evening's entertainment, I told him. Why would I have said that? What business was it of mine?

Bloomers? Was this a dream?

Later, I was informed that the fellow habitually forced himself on this somersaultist. For proof I'd been taken to look through the window of an adjoining bedroom as he pressed down upon her, flattening her out.

This was your dream, then.

You're eager for it to be a dream. If it was, it might have occurred after I saw Briony on the high bar. If it occurred before that, before I was even situated out west, it might not have been a dream. I've spent time in Eastern Europe, but how would you know that? I studied for a year in Prague. They had no money, the Czechs. They had mountainous Russia looking down at them. Their own secret police used to pop out of the bushes in powder blue jumpsuits and take your picture as you sat on a park bench. I spent time also in Hungary, in Budapest. There is a street there that World War II came through, first one way as the Germans advanced and the Russians retreated and then the other way as the Russians advanced and the Germans retreated. That one street for the war to flow back and forth through. And in a big lot there, near a high school, was a mass unmarked graveyard, skulls and femurs just under the sod. So it may not have been a dream. On the other hand I don't remember this somersault as you remember things in a specific context. Exactly where and when. So maybe it was a dream. All I can say is that I remember it as having a dark impoverished quality, like a flickering silent movie, and occurring in a shabby room with splintery floors and dirty windows, and so not something to have occurred even as a dream in the wide-open big-sky spaces of the democratic Far West. But the gymnastic linkage to Briony reminds me how far apart we were, not only in age and social position but in how we thought of our lives or, more exactly, our expectations of what life offered according to its nature as we understood it.

Who are we talking about now?

It was peculiar, to see something like an interior light on the face of this lovely brilliantly alive young college student, as a means of understanding my own shadowed existence some of which may have taken place in a shabby dance studio years before where I was taken to watch some woman in bloomers and undershirt turn herself into a flying missile.

Then you saw her again, the athletic college student?

She had a name, you know.

Briony.

My wife-to-be.

On the first day of his elementary Brain Science class, Andrew was writing his name on the blackboard when the chalk snapped in two. "And—" was as far as he'd gotten, and when he turned to look for the errant piece of chalk that had flown past his ear he knocked his lectern awry so that the books he had placed on it slid to the floor. He heard student laughter. And then Briony, in this bright fluorescent classroom with mountains watching through the window, rose from her chair in the first row and picked up the books and the piece of chalk. She was not bluejeaned like the others, she wore a long pale-yellow frock with shoulder straps and the running shoes they all wore. The combination made him smile. She was a slender wheat-haired beauty with the fairest skin, as if a property of it was sunlight. Andrew thanked her for her kindness and proceeded with the lecture. She sat with her running shoes pointed at each other under that long dress and her head bent over her notebook computer as she typed her notes, a serious student, listening with her head bowed over her chair-desk. He thought of her legs under that dress.

And then he realized this was the girl on the high bar.

Good morning, class. *Good morning, pale-yellow shift and running shoes.* Today we begin our exploration of consciousness, the field of all meaning, the necessary and sufficient condition of language, the beginning of all good mornings. Consciousness—*not what that heavy-lidded lout slumped in the chair next to you confronts the world with, but* what is left when you erase all presumptions, forgo your affections, white out the family, school, church, and nation in which you have couched your being . . . cast off the techno clutter of civilization, cut the wires of all circuits, including connections to your internal mechanisms, your bowel conditions, your hungers, what itches, what bleeds or produces tears, or the cracklings in the joints when you rise from a sitting position, *abandon, however reluctantly, your breathless lips-apart contemplation of me, how my voice resonates in you, how my glance lases your netherness,* and float free and unconnected in your own virtual black and starless space. And thus you have nothing to fix on, nothing for your thought to adhere to, no image, no sound, no smell, no physical sensation of any kind. You are not in a place, you are the place. You are not here, you are everywhere. You are not in relation to anything else. There is no anything else. There is nothing you can think of except of yourself thinking. You are in the depthless dingledom of your own soul.

O lovely acrobat, it is true we may be immaterial presences in our beings, mere currents in the ocean of our molecules. But take heart! Let your wild desires bring you back to earth, to culture, to citizenship, to your bodily needs. To me. I have so much to teach you! And love is the blunt concussion that renders us insensible to despair.

This doesn't sound like the Andrew I know.

I'm another man in front of a class.

So you were smitten.

Well, I admit I was vulnerable. But she was truly glorious. Something happens in the heart, you know. You recognize life as it should be. And so what you thought of as life were only the shadows in the cave.

What cave?

You've never read your Plato, Doc. Where most people live, most of us, imagining it to be the real sunlit world when it is only a cave lit by the flickering fires of illusion. Briony was out there in the sun. I began as a horny lecher, instantly evolved into a worshipful adorer, and then, as it turned really bad, I felt that I couldn't live without her.

Good morning, class. *Good morning pink knee and peek of cursive underthigh in her short denim skirt today.*

27

You may have assumed from our last lecture that my argument was only theoretical, that of course there is no existence without the world, and thus no mind apart from its engagement with the world. Consciousness without world is impossible, just as there is no sight without the light to see by. Is that your objection, *my darling? Bent over her notebook, her face framed in the fall of hair.* Well, then, let's look at this solid real world of yours. It has a platform in space and that platform has a history of animate life. So far so good. But notice, there does not seem to be a necessary or sufficient condition for animacy, it occurs under any conditions. You would think it needs air, but it does not, you would think it needs to see or hear or lope, or swim or fly or hang by its tail from a tree branch, but it does not. It requires no particular shape or size or any particular supplies from the mineral universe in order to be life, it can make itself out of anything. It can live underwater or on a mote of dust, in ice or in boiling seawater, it may have eyes or ears but may not, it may have the means to ingest but may not, or the means to move about but may not, it may have a procreative organ but may not, it may be sentient but may not, and even when it has intelligence may not have it in sufficiency, *as for example the nodding sloth who always manages to be sitting next to you—who when he yawns his eyes disappear, have you noticed that, my lo-*

ganberry? So life is taxonomically without limit but with one intention common to its endless varieties—be they fish, fly, dung beetle, mite, worm, or bacterium—one intention to define it in all its minded or mindless manifestations—its pathetic intention to survive. Because of course it never does, *does it, my bosky babe,* for if life is one definable thing of infinite form then we have to say it feeds on itself. It is self-consuming. And that is not very reassuring if you mean to depend on the world for your consciousness. Is it? If consciousness exists without the world, it is nothing, and if it needs the world to exist, it is still nothing.

These were my preparatory thought experiments—to begin from a basic philosophical hopelessness before looking for rescue from the first responders, Emerson, William James, Damasio, and the rest. But I must have given myself away as nothing more than a depressive.

Who was the lout?

He was no contest, really. Long, lean, indolent, with black hair combed back wet, like Tarzan. The school's star quarterback. He didn't stand a chance once I entered the picture.

And "bosky babe"?

Yes, that was a momentary lapse, a lingering thought

of my high school girlfriend who was the bosky babe down there. Not Briony. Briony, for comfort's sake as she did her spandex-suited gymnastics, kept her mons trimmed.

There were a lot of western blondes at the college but mostly of the blaringly self-indicative kind, with an empty-headedness or cunning about them, or perhaps their faces too clearly anticipated cosmetic collapse. Briony was fine-featured, her looks were modestly aristocratic, you would think she belonged at a country house in the Cotswolds or perhaps in a Polish shtetl. For some reason I kept seeing her around the campus. Riding her bike, standing in the cafeteria line, talking with friends. Didn't that mean something? Each time she arrived for class she smiled hello. I asked her if she would volunteer to be a subject for the lab work and she said yes. And so, one morning, as I placed the electrode net on her pretty head—didn't shave it, of course, this was not medical science, just a way to show the electric busyness of our brains—I had reason to tuck her long hair behind her ears. I inhaled the clean freshness of her. I felt I was in a sunlit meadow. I did a basic brain graph using an old EEG machine I had brought west with me. Something like a lie detector, very primitive, but useful for Brain Science 101. Flashing pictures at her, seeing where the graph spiked, where she was frightened, where she remembered something, where she was hungry, where a sexual innuendo lit her up. The exercise was illustrative, this was elementary stuff, nothing about localizations. The other students stood around and watched and made jokes. The lout was there with a stupidly superior smile on his face. I decided I would flunk him, not that it would matter. But I saw things the students couldn't have. I saw things more intimately Briony's than if I had seen her undressed. This wasn't mere voyeurism, it was cephalic-invasive, I admit, but, after all, less legitimate scientific inference than professorial fantasy.

What did you see?

One of the flash cards was a picture of a toy circus. A one-ring circus with a circus master in top hat and jodhpurs in the center and ladies in tutus standing on backs of ponies galloping in a circle around the ring and overhead a man in tights hanging upside down from a trapeze and a woman in matching tights suspended from his hands. That practically took the pen off the scroll. It actually made me uneasy that the joys of a child were still evocative.

And then the despair of my chosen field. You've got to be brave when you do science. I reacted badly to the publication of an experiment demonstrating that the brain can come to a decision seconds before we're conscious of it.

That is unsettling. And you disagree?

It would be easy to disagree. Say "Wait a minute. Is this duplicable? Will it stand?" But my own brain took over and declared its solidarity with the experiment's results. There will be more sophisticated experiments and it will be established that free will is an illusion.

But surely—

One morning I found myself abandoning my lecture and blurting out something I had not planned to say— something like a preamble to a course in cognitive science that I had not yet devised. . . . [*thinking*]

What did you say?

What?

Something you blurted out to the class.

I asked this question: How can I think about my brain when it's my brain doing the thinking? So is this brain pretending to be me thinking about it? I can't trust anyone these days, least of all myself. I am a mysteriously generated consciousness, and no comfort to me that it's one of billions. That's what I said to them and then picked up my books and walked out of the room.

Hmmm.

What do you mean "Hmmm"? You remember why the great Heinrich von Kleist committed suicide? He'd read Kant, who said we could never know reality. He should have come out west, Heinrich. Would have saved his life. No despair of intellect possible in these parts. Something about the mountains and the sky. Something about the football team.

So you were an anomaly with your intellectual crisis.

Only one student showed up for the next class and that was Briony. We went to the student union and had coffee. She was concerned, looked me over with a compassionate frown. As I see her now I realize that she never fussed with herself the way young women do, running their hands through their hair, tieing it back if it's loose, letting it loose if it's tied, all those small gestures of self-reflection. Briony did nothing of that sort, she sat still, calmly present in the moment with no undercurrent of self-regard. This was early enough in the semester for students to drop out of one class and switch to another and she knew that could mean trouble for me. Of course the dean would get on my back but I couldn't have cared less with this glorious creature before me. I basked in her sympathy. I wore a mournful expression. She extended her hand across the table as if to console me. She did not want to show me that she found me strange. She was the sort of person who'd feel obliged to engage a leper in conversation.

What was her background?

Her background? The Wasatch mountains.

No, I mean—

You want to know where she was from, this extraordinary child, who her parents were, the family that produced her?

Yes.

Why does that matter? They don't tell you in movies where people grew up unless the movies are about people growing up. They never tell you where your heroes come from, to whom they were related, you just find them as they are, in the present moment. You're called to worry about them as they live on the screen and all you know about them is the time they're there. No history, no past, just them.

Is this a movie?

This is America. Having discovered each other we went hiking in the mountains, Briony and I. You could walk right up the street and find yourself at the foot of a mountain trail. The Wasatch let you know they were always there—even when your back was turned, even as you drove away from them, you sensed them. They

changed constantly according to the light they negotiated but also the temperature, their coloration like their
change of mood, but they were constant presences, a
family of gods, low mountains jagged in the peaks,
this one taller, that one shorter, but all connected, an
alliance of venerable powers, trail-scarred, implacable
with snow that could kill, or carelessly alive with spring
foliage in all the pale shades of green or blue evergreen,
but still with the yellow-brown remnants of the previous year. And then their tilt, their rising backward to
their apex in the sky as if in aversion to something we
supplicants had done to displease them, for when you
lived in that town awhile you knew those mountains
ruled, they walled you in, you were their people. Briony
in her white shorts with her belted water bottle and
baseball cap with the blond hair ponytailed through the
hole in back, and her hiking boots and ankle socks and
firm rounded mulping calves—Briony climbed ahead of
me, and she was vigorous, and in my need to keep up—
at moments I worried that she was trying to get away
from me—I could not luxuriate in contemplation of
her legs and the glory of her tight white shorts as she
hoisted herself over rocks, sometimes touching the
ground for support, or gripping an outcrop, and so
climbing higher and higher, the path more like a series
of cryptic Tibetan steps into a Buddhist acceptance of

the way things really were when you didn't talk about them.

Well, I was only asking.

You lack empathy, you don't know when to stop asking me these things. You can't imagine what it was like having her but never forgetting for a moment my killing ineptitude. That I would be at my most dangerous when blissfully happy. How I had to concentrate moment by moment, examine my actions, everything I did, living attentively with the minutiae, watching myself every waking minute, attending carefully, ritualistically, to everything I did so as not to become Andrew the Pretender. I can't talk to you anymore, it is too painful. You don't get it. Just speaking her name destroys me. I can no longer hear her voice.

You, with the ear for voices?

I can still summon the voices of my long-dead mother and father. I can hear their voices quite well if only for a fading moment. What I hear is their moral nature. My mother's practicality. My father's sad evasiveness. Their moral nature is in the remembered voices of the dead. It is what is left of the dead that is still them, that fragment of the voice that renders a moral nature though the rest of the person is gone.

But her voice, Briony's voice, is gone, you say? You don't hear it? Maybe that's why for my part I can't seem to get a fix on her. I get your voice, your feeling what you think and feel about her. It's as if it's in the way, your voice. What was she like, except for her athleticism? And she was a math major? They go together, perhaps, the math, the gymnastics. Doing geometry on the parallel bars.

Who said she was a math major? How did you know that?

Didn't you say—?

Are you CIA?

Really, Andrew.

I don't know why I talk to you.

Martha I feel as if I know from your description of the way she acted. But Briony doesn't come through to me.

She was a younger person, Briony, still becoming herself. Innocently smart. Unaffected. She didn't act as if she felt especially pretty. She was intensely physical, as grown children are. When she liked something it was passionately. She had favorite books, favorite bands. She worked at her studies. She could write a grammatical sentence—you know how rare that is in an undergraduate? She believed in her life, her future.

I see.

Martha was being, Briony was becoming. What kind of a shrink are you who has to be told this? You have the heartlessness of someone living vicariously. That's what you're doing, isn't it, living vicariously through me. I am grist for your mill. Jesus! Don't you have a life of your own?

Not really.

I'm not clear on the time here. When did you and Briony marry?

We never married.

She was your wife.

Of course she was my wife, but we never married. We never got around to it. We never got past the intense feeling for each other that you have to get past in order to legally marry. In our minds we were married. We didn't need anyone else to tell us we were. We were Andy and Bri. One day I went to the Saturday football game, and there she was, of course, atop the cheerleader pyramid, and doing a swan dive into all their arms at the end of the cheer.

I should have known . . .

Meanwhile there *he* was, the lout, padded and helmeted, leading his team out of the huddle, glancing disdainfully at the defenders, running off his plays with calm authority and moving his team efficiently down the field. I watched as he threw the football forty yards in the air, a perfect spiral right into the arms of his receiver. Touchdown. Twenty thousand people leapt to their feet, and roared, the college band struck up a victory march, some idiot in an ape costume danced a jig in front of the stands, and I realized I had stepped into a powerful tribal culture here, and if I was going to extract her from it I had some thinking to do.

I seem to recall your saying the lout didn't have a chance once you entered the picture.

Well, after all, I was Andrew, he of the dark mournful eyes. Even as I lectured provocatively, they shone with a glistening cry for help. To Briony this was personhood on display. The vulnerability of the teacher at the lectern was a new classroom experience for her. She stared at me, she was attentive. [*thinking*] I'd known since high school that women were attracted to me. My first girlfriend was a zoology nerd at the Bronx High School of Science. She said I had the eyes of a langur. After school we went to her apartment, where her parents weren't home, and we made out.

Because of your languorous eyes.

Well, that and the mop of curly hair, though by now it has lost its color. I have always been good-looking in a kind of weak-jawed way. And I had attitude. I was one of those wise-ass high school kids, loose-limbed and scornful of everything. The fact is, Doc, that I've had a lot of success with women. But this with Briony was different. Overwhelming. An abrupt neural resetting wherein I found myself with an immense capacity for love. Much later, when we were living together—actually, we had gone out for a celebratory dinner—we had just learned that she was pregnant—Briony admitted to a revolutionary experience of her own: Andy, she said, I realized one day in class that I'd been waiting for you. And there you were. There was such recognition. It was as if this was only the latest of our lives, she said.

But at this point, here at the peak of the Wasatches, I only knew how I felt. It wouldn't do to be careless. I needed to know more before making my move. More of what, I didn't know. [*thinking*]

What?

Emil Jannings.

What?

I didn't want to be Emil Jannings in *The Blue Angel*. You remember that movie? The professor who falls in love with this cabaret singer Marlene Dietrich and ends up as a clown in her sleazy act, crowing "Cock-a-doodle-doo!" He gives up everything to marry her and of course she screws around. His life is ruined, job, dignity, it's all gone. He staggers back to his empty classroom one night and dies at his desk. You mean you never saw that?

No.

At least he had his desk.

Of course Briony could not be compared to a decadent Weimar cabaret singer. On the other hand I knew I could accomplish whatever it took to destroy myself. I could imagine her staring at me in a kind of end-of-it-all sorrow as I did the Far West equivalent of a cock-a-doodle-doo dive off the mountaintop. As we sat to catch our, or rather my, breath, and drank our bottled water, I said to her, Briony, not many people could have persuaded me to climb up here.

But, Professor, it's good and aren't you glad you did? Don't you feel happy? Because a climb like this gets the good brain hormones going.

I said: Please don't call me Professor, call me Andrew. That's what the other students call me, after all.

She smiled. OK, I will, then. Andrew. I don't know what to make of you, Pro— I mean Andrew. I've never met anyone like you before.

Howso, I said.

I don't know. I'm not bored with you. No, that isn't the word, I'm not bored in my life, I've got too much to do to be bored—

That was true, she had her classes, her gymnastics, her cheerleading, she waited table in the faculty dining room and on weekends she put in hours at a local old people's home.

—but your moodiness, she said, I don't know, that's

so unusual, a powerful thing, almost like your way of life. And it's such a personal way to be up in front of a class. It almost seems like a strength, like someone who has an affliction and is brave about it. When it's just, I don't know, a worldview that's very solemn.

And I said: Briony, I think if we carry this as far as I'd like to, I will end up depressing you into marrying me.

Oh, how she laughed! And I with her. At that moment we were no longer teacher and student. She must have realized this because she grew quiet, not looking at me. She made a ceremonious thing of unscrewing her water bottle and holding it to her lips. I detected the faintest flush on her throat. [*thinking*]

Yes? You were saying?

No, I was just thinking. Suppose there was a computer network more powerful than anything we could imagine.

What's this?

I remember trying this idea out on her. And never mind a network, just this one awesome computer, say. And because it was what it was, suppose it had the capacity to record and store the acts and thoughts and feelings of every living person on earth once around per millisecond of time. I mean, as if all of existence was data for this computer—as if it was a storehouse of all the deeds ever done, the thoughts ever thought, the feelings ever felt. And since the human brain contains memories, this computer would record these as well, and so be going back in time through the past even as it went forward with the present.

That is a tall order, even for a computer.

Not for this baby. Consider the possibility that there are things you don't know, Doc.

I consider that every day.

I'll tell you one thing you may not know: The genome of every human cell has memory. You know what that means? As evolved beings we have in our genes memories of the far past, of long-ago generations, memories of experiences not our own. This is not pie-in-the-sky stuff, a neuroscientist will tell you the same thing. And all we need is the right code to extract what the cell knows, what it remembers.

Sounds poetic.

I'm talking science here, I'm telling you my computer to end all computers that sucks up the mental and physical activities of every living thing—I mean, let's throw in the animals too—necessarily then can go back in time and move into the past as readily as it moves along with the present. Do you give me that?

OK, Andrew.

So what that means, what that means . . .

Yes?

. . . that at least on the microgenetic level couldn't there be the possibility of recomposing a whole person from these bits and pieces and genomic memories of lives past?

You don't mean cloning.

No, dammit, I don't mean cloning. We're talking about how this computer could crack the code of every cell of every human brain and reconstitute the dead from their experiences. Isn't that something like reincarnation? Maybe it wouldn't be perfect, you couldn't always see her, maybe if you reached out she would be just a shade of herself, but she would be a presence, and the love would be there.

Who are we speaking of now?

What possessed me to tell Briony all this? If this computer could come up with the code to read the makeup of our cells, in birth, in death, in the ashes of our cremation, in the rot of our coffins, and of course it could because of what it was, then we could recover our lost babies, our lost lovers, our lost selves, bring them back from the dead, reunite in a kind of heaven on earth. Do you see that?

Well, maybe on a speculative level . . .

But if you accept the premise the logic is sound, will you give me that?

I give you that.

44

But you still don't know what this computer is, do you? Oh, Doc, if there was such a computer, it could do anything, finally. I mean, call it by its rightful name. And I could have my baby with Martha brought back. And I could have my Briony, and we would bring our baby home and we would be a family.

II

You asked me to keep a diary or daybook. Writing is like talking to yourself, which I have been doing with you all along anyway, Doc. So what's the difference. I'm writing from Down East: This morning it's like the winter fog has frozen. To walk the fields is to feel yourself breasting the air, leaving behind you the sound of tinkling ice and a tubular indication of your form. But I need places like this. I am safe here. I mean, for all we know I put you in danger every time I walk into your office.

And now, later, the wind has come up and blows snow against my window and I must turn on the light. I have nothing to read here but the cabin owner's complete works of Mark Twain, MT embossed on the cracked binding. How MT dealt with life was to make a point of explaining children to adults, and adults to children. Isn't that so? Or to write of his neighbors with amused compassion. He went to ridiculous church for the sake of his wife. Invested in an unworkable Linotype machine. Hobnobbed with the Brahmins of Boston. Slyly skewered the self-satisfied gentlemen enjoying his after-dinner speeches. Noted the anointed barbarity of kings. But always, always, it was to wrap himself in society. To keep himself snugly within what Searle, a guy whose work I teach, calls "the construction of social reality."

And just now, loud as a clap of thunder, a poor dumb gull riding the winds has bashed his head against the windowpane. I exchange looks with his glazed eye as he slides a smeared red funnel down the snow on my window.

Another day: I see through the fog the humped green heron, out there on the piling. All huddled into himself, a gloom bird, one of us.

Now, later, the sky turned cold and clear, the wind cuffing the seawater, and I imagine a warm swamp somewhere filled with the jumping frogs of Calaveras County. I mean, you read him and he does put one over. But for me the intemperate ghost of MT rises from his folksy childhood and rages at the imperial monster he has helped create.

I see his frail grasp of life at those moments of his prose, his after-dinner guard let down and his upwardly mobile decency become vulnerable to his self-creation. And the woman he loved, gone, and a child he loved, gone, and he looks in the mirror and hates the pretense of his white hair and mustache and suit, all gathered in the rocking-chair wisdom that resides in his bleary eyes. He despairs of the likelihood that the world is his illusion, that he is but a vagrant mind in a futile drift through eternity.

See the ant, he says, how stupid and incompetent he is, dragging some fly's wing hither and yon, hauling it over pebbles because they are in his way, climbing leaves of grass because he doesn't know not to, and where does he think he's going, says MT, nowhere, that's where.

Another morning. I am down on the beach as the osprey hovers pulsingly over the sea, and the sanderlings tiptoe along the ocean's foamy edge while the shadowing bluefish waits for the tide to flip them into its razored maw.

This is you, God. And who did you say it was, Jonah, riding the struts of the leviathan? With the tons of fish washing beneath him into the digestive caldron, as he plants one foot on one beamy rib, the other on the other, and it would be dark except for the luminescence of the electric fishes looking to find their way out, against the tide, against the moon-rock slurp of the ocean tide, against the diurnal twist of the rumbling planet that cups the ocean, that nods the mountains back and forth in metronomic rhythm . . .

. . . this earth we find ourselves gravity-stuck to, me and MT and my flaxen-haired fairy-tale beauty, my darling who read to me, by the light of a flashlight, as I drove us at night across the continent, read to me of the imperial outrages annotated by MT in the last years of his life, when the truth of his humor turned green and bilious, when he saw by the light of the moon with the night heron humpslunk between its shoulders that the impossible world was not effectively met any longer by satire or mockery.

So, Doc, I write to tell you that I agree: Life—in being irresolute, forever unfinished though the deaths are astronomical—is not a movie. I do not see in my mind a white-robed D-cup empress facing down a phalanx of centurions looking like me in their spiked helmets and shields and spears and leather-striped calves, those extra-filled movies that drip their Technicolor effusions over the ghosts of the ancient empire so like our own.

Ah, but when they didn't make a sound, how uncanny they were with the title cards doing the talking, the written-out words blocking our view to make things clearer. A mysterious intervening translation agency connecting us in our own language to a shadow world where humans like us were speaking to one another in their spiked helmets and shields, in their black ties and cigarette holders and ass-clinging white satin evening gowns, but from such otherwordly distances that you could not hear them, though they seemed to hear themselves.

How goddamn awful, so much of life having been a wasteful expenditure of time, of living not bravely or at home on the planet of delights, of thunderous icebergs calving, tsunamis rinsing away the seacoasts, of drought withering the cornfields, not at home in any of that, or atop mountains or on the sea but in cities only, a person seated in the subway car amid a carful of subway persons, or running under an umbrella to the available cab, or going to the theater or listening to Mahler or reading the news and not doing anything about it . . . that news that always seemed to happen to other people in other places. Except when it happened to me. When it finally happened to me . . .

Very interesting, Andrew. Surprising.

Yeah, well, I'm another man when I'm alone in a cabin.

I had almost given up on you.

I don't know what I'm doing here.

I can tell you that, as a boy one winter afternoon, Andrew appeared at the door of his little girlfriend to return the doll he'd stolen from her. His mother had insisted that he do this, knock on the door and not give any excuse, or suggest he'd found it in the street or anything that wasn't the truth, but just to say he'd taken the doll when she wasn't looking and he was sorry and would never do anything like that again. Andrew did as he was told. The little girl took the doll out of his hands and slammed the door in his face. On the way home he slipped on a patch of ice and broke his eyeglasses.

This was where?

Montcalm, New Jersey. A town not as well-to-do as Glen Vale, its neighbor. Old two- and three-story houses, some with glassed-in porches and most with patchy untended front yards and needing paint jobs behind the worn-out trees lining the streets. You can tell you'd passed over into Glen Vale when everything was brighter, the front yards groomed, the trees full and rich-looking, the homes bigger with more space between them. America will always tell you how much money people have.

Why did you steal the doll?

For a physical examination. It was a girl doll and I needed to confirm what I suspected.

You wore glasses as a child?

I've always been nearsighted. Why are you asking these questions? I'm trying to tell you something. My life was discordant. I was usually in one sort of trouble or another. Do you know what belly flopping is? You hold the sled in front of you, start running, and when you're up to speed you fling yourself down on the sled and you're off.

On your Flexible Flyer.

Good, Doc, so you're in this world after all. There weren't any real hills in Montcalm, my street went along as a gently descending tilt, and so we used our driveways for momentum, that was our practice, taking advantage of their slight elevation, belly flopping halfway down the driveway and twisting the sled handle to make a right turn once we cleared it. If you turned too sharply the sled went over on its side and dumped you. So I didn't make too sharp a turn this time I'm speaking of, but did it by degrees till I was still in my turn halfway across to the other sidewalk. The other thing to mention, it was dusk, the time you should have been home. Your cheeks were red, your nose was dripping water, snow clung to your eyebrows, snow was under your sleeves and inside your boots. A horn blew. I looked up into the toothy grille of a Buick sedan. The guy had braked, and the car spun in a neat circle around me backward, three hundred and sixty degrees. It was like an act of some sort, first he was behind me then he was in front of me, all the time spinning around backward. Then I heard a big bong, as the car slammed into a light pole down the street. All this time the man had been pounding on his horn, it was a brassy tritone horn, as if to announce a festive event, but now with the car crashed it was an anticlimactic continuous blare, very unpleasant. I saw that he had hit the light pole hard enough for it to be slightly askew. I got off my sled and went closer. He had hit the pole on the driver's side, and what was blowing the horn was his head, resting on the steering wheel while his hands hung down beside him. OK?

OK.

We moved to New York, Greenwich Village. My father said it was because we'd be closer to his job at NYU. But I knew it was because our family was persona non grata in Montcalm after that crash. I said as much and my father said, Son, lots of kids were sleigh riding and it could have been any one of them in the path of that car. It just happened to be you. He didn't believe this any more than I did. He knew that if any kid was likely to cause a fatal crash it would be me.

You father was an academic?

He did science. Molecular biology. He said science was like a searchlight beam growing wider and wider and illuminating more and more of the universe. But as the beam widened so did the circumference of darkness.

I thought Albert Einstein said that.

I was lonely in the city and had no friends and so my

parents got me a dog, a dachshund. They said it was my responsibility to care for it, walk it, train it to obey. That was interesting, trying to see what kind of a brain it had. Not much was the answer. It had a nose that seemed to serve as a brain. The nose/brain's primary function of course was to process smell. Because I had that dog I noticed all the other dogs in the park and they all went around smelling one another and the urological codes they left at the base of water fountains, tree trunks, chess tables, and so on. What they did with these signals was nothing that I could see. Maybe it was just a kind of conversation. Or like emails. They'd compute the olfactory signal, pee out their response, and walk on. This was Washington Square Park, and lots of people came there with their dogs. There was a dog run, like everything else in the city a measured space for whatever you wanted to do.

You sound like a confirmed New Yorker.

My puppy with its short legs tried to get into the game on that run. It was funny to see him waddling after some big dog who turned and ran past him the other way before he could turn his sausage of a body around.

What did you name your dog?

I hadn't gotten around to that. I was finding out that I didn't respect him all that much. I mean, you couldn't insult him, which was a sign of his mental deficiency. He would never take offense no matter what I said to him or how I yanked on the leash. So in this time I'm speaking of, I was walking him home one afternoon through the park—we had a university apartment on the west side of the Square. More trees on that side, which made it darker, quieter, there were fewer people. This is not a Tom Sawyer episode I'm about to relate.

I rather thought that.

I saw something under a bench that looked like a Spaldeen, a valuable pink rubber ball. I wasn't sure. I got down on my knees to investigate, poking my hand under the bench, and that's when I must have let go of the leash. Next thing I knew my dog let out a cry, a tenor squeal— a weird unnatural sound from a dog—and when I looked around I saw his leash waving about in the air. I didn't question why but grabbed for it—an automatic reflex— and felt transmitted to my arm, as if it was my own pounding pulse, the wing beat of the hawk that had him. That's what it was, a red-tailed hawk. You would think I could have yanked the dog loose, maybe bringing the hawk down too unless it released the creature, but its talons were dug into the dachshund's neck and for a moment I was given to understand implacable nature. [*thinking*] Yes, I was in touch with an insistent rhythmic force, mindless and without personality. For a moment I held the hawk suspended, as it beat its wings while unable to rise. I won't swear to it but I think I was actually lifted to my toes before I let go and watched the bird shoot up to the top of a tree, the leash hanging down like a vine, my dachshund immobile in shock as the bird pressed its neck onto the branch and pecked at its eyes.

Why did you let go, was the hawk too strong for you? How old were you at this time?

Seven, eight, I don't know. But I try to remember at what point I felt it was no use. Was I too frightened to hold on? Did I understand it was all over for the dog the moment those talons curled into him? I'm not sure. Perhaps, deferential to God's world, I had merely conceded. I stepped back to get a better view of what was happening up in the tree. The hawk didn't look down, our struggle had been of no consequence to him, he was tearing into the little dog as if I didn't exist. I can remember the thrill of feeling the pulse of those wings in my skinny little chest. Nevertheless, I ran home crying. It was all my fault. There you have it. Early Andrew. I'm presuming you like childhoods.

Well, they can be instructive.

The day before we took off for California, Briony found a stray mutt and insisted on taking it with us. Speaking of dogs.

When was this?

Lots of dogs on the campus whose student owners let them run loose and finally forgot them. She said this one looked so appealingly at her that she couldn't resist. A big black-and-white dog, with floppy ears. It stood with its paws on the back of my seat and its wet nose nuzzled my neck as I tried to drive.

Why were you going to California?

She named it Pete. He's a Pete, don't you think?, she said. She had turned around, her knees on the front seat, as she leaned over my shoulder to pet the damn thing. Yes, she said, that's your name all right.

Here I was in a state of such possessive love that I couldn't bear to share Briony with anyone else, not even a stupid mutt. I wanted her exclusive attention. I didn't say anything but I felt resentful, as if I had been invited to accompany her with no more thought on her part than she had impulsively bestowed on the dog.

Why were you going to California?

And it didn't help that the lout bid us goodbye, or bid *her* goodbye, there on the sidewalk in front of his dorm.

Did the lout have a name?

I don't know. Duke something. What else could it have been? She kissed him lightly on the mouth and touched his cheek and got in the car and closed the door and looked back and waved as I drove off. A voice in my mind said, "Step on it!" What the hero says to the cabbie in every 1930s movie. That voice in my head defining the moment: I was not of this generation. I was not of their time. I did not have this girl by any legitimate right.

Surely she had some choice in the matter.

I'm telling you how I felt. Briony knew I was divorced but no more than that. I had wanted to be completely open with her but I couldn't bring myself to tell her everything. Clearly, I had become her project.

Her project? So you still didn't understand how taken she was.

I sensed her interest. I felt indulged. I couldn't believe more than that. Not that I was without guile. The gloomier I was the more attentive she was. This had gone on through the semester. I could affect my nihilistic despair, making a lie even of that, I could wear the appropriate face while inside of myself I was smiling like an idiot. It was all I could do to keep my hands off her. But she was picking up my language, she was reading the course work, so that every boldly thoughtful sentence that came from her I could credit to my teaching. Briony had the intellectual assertiveness of the young, who make the learned ideas their own. She even mentioned the brain's limbic system and looked at me with a question in her eyes. I had instantly to get her off of that.

Why?

Damage to the limbic system inhibits feeling, among other things. There's indifference, coolness. You're half alive. People who've been traumatized show limbic system dysfunction.

Do you believe you suffered such an experience? Had you been traumatized?

Only by life. Listen, when I was with Briony there was nothing wrong with my limbic system. My hippocampus and my amygdala were up and running. Whistling, applauding. Doing back flips. Fortunately, my course syllabus included readings from William James, Dewey, Rorty, and then the French existentialists, Sartre, Camus. She dove into all that.

For a course in elementary brain science?

Well, it was over most of their heads. And what they understood they didn't like. I wasn't aware of any particular religiosity among these kids, it was more that God was an assumption, like something preinstalled in their computers. But if there was a philosophy that was appropriate to the study of the brain, of the material of consciousness, I maintained it was either pragmatism or existentialism. Or maybe both. No God in either, you see. No soul. No metaphysical bullshit. Briony got it. But for her, a little more drama and human exaltation was in the idea of a painful freedom. So she opted for the existentialists. And applied her knowledge like a pragmatist to me. The evidence was clear that I was of the existentialist school. That I was outside the realm of psychology—I had an historic identity. That seemed to make fast the connection between us. She was happy with Andrew the Existentialist. She could kiss me on the cheek. She could find me in my office and come in with two coffees. I wanted to get down on my knees and kiss the hem of her frock. This clean lovely creature of the West had found in what she decided was my existentialism the resurrection of the nineteenth-century Romantic—Andrew poised at cliff's edge with the back of his hand pressed to his brow.

It was just a matter of time before we became lovers. The first time, it was in her dorm room. She took her clothes off and lay down and turned her face to the wall while I undressed. Migod, to hold this tremulous being in my arms. After that she always rode her bike to my place. . . . And I remember when she woke me up one dawn, dragging me out of bed like an excited child, and pulling me stumbling up the stairs to the roof of my suite motel to watch the rising sun light the mountaintops. I doubt that my seduction technique had ever before been practiced in this country of cowboys. I had taken her out of her time, out of her place, and I was jealous even of the stray dog that she'd picked up to come with us on our trip.

So as I understand it, you were going to California

with the girl of your dreams and what with one thing or another you managed to feel miserable about it.

We were off to see her parents. How would you feel?

Briony directed Andrew to a little seaside town about an hour south of Los Angeles. He turned off the Coast Highway to a street lined with small-scale homes in pastel colors. The predominating building material was stucco. In front of each home, a garden patch stuffed with ridiculously exorbitant tropical plants in flower. Perhaps he was tired from the two days on the road. Even Briony's excitement as she pointed him to one of the narrow driveways that separated each house from its neighbor he found annoying. And who was this running up to the front door, flinging it open and disappearing inside— certainly not the spectacular spandexed handstander on the high bar, nor the lovely creature demurely submitting to a brain scan in the elementary cognitive science lab, nor the lover of an older man. Coming home for some-one her age was a regression to childhood. Andrew stood by the car with his hands on his hips and looked over the neighborhood. It was shadowless. Heat shimmering from the white pavement. He couldn't admit to himself how nervous he felt, how out of place, squiring this child like some vile seducer.

I can understand this was a difficult moment for you.

Yes. I didn't want to follow her. The house was just a short walk from a retaining wall at the end of the street. I found myself looking down a vine-covered hillside to a beach covered with people—a brueghel of people, sunning themselves, playing volleyball, children picking up shells along the water's edge. More of them were out in the blue water drifting patiently on their surfboards. Beyond was the Pacific, flecked with sailboats. Above it all, in a smoggy sky, was a bloodstained sun clearly intending to set over the sea. The whole scene seemed unnatural. Where I come from the sun sets over the land.

Briony was calling to him from the house, waving, smiling. He turned and noticed the parents' car that he had parked behind, a red Morris Minor. You didn't see many of those anymore. At the door, Briony took his hand. They're out back, she said. And in the short walk through the house to the garden Andrew had the impression of—what to call it—a prosthetic house? The stairway to the second floor was made of shallow half steps, the upholstered chairs and sofa in the living room had attached footstools. The center island in the kitchen was stepped. Whatever needed to be used came with graduated access, handrails. And the place smelled very clean, antiseptic almost. All of this Andrew perceived peripherally as he passed through the house and to the garden where there, smiling and rising to greet him, and not crippled or maimed at all, were Briony's parents. I'm Bill, he said. I'm Betty, she said.

The fact that I was a college teacher was in my favor. These were retired show-business people with great respect for the education they never had. And so loving of their daughter that they trusted her judgment. Never even a raised eyebrow for this man twice their daughter's age. Gave me a hearty welcome. So I had worried for no reason. There were bottles and an ice bucket on a tea caddy. You name it we got it, Bill said. We had drinks, Briony sitting close to me on the settee, glancing at me for my reaction. But Bill and Betty were classy, they had the social ease of longtime performers. They were young-looking given that they were retirees. It's hard to tell with Diminutives.

Diminutives?

You don't want to patronize them. "Midgets" is beyond the pale. Derives from the insect the midge. And "Little People" is not much better.

You're saying Briony's parents were midgets?

Only out of their hearing.

My goodness. And "Diminutives" was their term of choice?

That's my term. They didn't speak of themselves descriptively. You just look at them and you go into the politically correct mode. To my credit I didn't even blink the moment I saw them. Just an example of the brain's synaptic speed. It had probably told me what I'd find as I'd walked through the house.

Why hadn't Briony warned you?

I don't know. Could she have been testing me? My reaction a measure of my character? But it couldn't have been that. Briony was incapable of any kind of subterfuge. And she was too self-aware to act unconsciously. And why should she warn me? We were seriously together—why would something like that matter? They were her folks, who were in her sight lines from the day she was born. She loved them. And given their sociability with others of their like she was raised in an aura of normality, not being the only child in that situation. You don't go around apologizing for your mom and dad.

But what young girl of even normally proportioned parents will not say something in advance by way of softening their effect? A parent is a person who embarrasses you.

Well, this was Briony. This was the girl who led me up the mountain. She was in all ways enigmatic. I was deeply in the world of her affections—why wouldn't I know already, without being told, that her parents were tiny?

What can I say that will satisfy you? En route to CA, she gave her dog away to some kid who worked at the motel where we stayed one night. At the time, I didn't know why she would do that—after impulsively bringing it along, naming it Pete, and then giving him away to someone, and with a dollar or two to buy some kibble. She knelt and hugged the dog and looked on sadly as the kid walked him away on a leash. Perhaps that was the acknowledgment you're looking for. When I saw Briony take her mother in her arms and hold her as you would a child, when I watched her kneeling to hug her father, I could see why she might have had second thoughts about Pete the dog. He was big. Had a tail on him that could crack your fibula.

I just remembered—she did tell me one thing, Briony. She asked me not to talk politics with her father. My last-minute instructions. We were just approaching the family manse. She kissed my cheek. Oh, and, Andrew, please, please, no politics, OK?

What was that about?

We were in Orange County, CA, the land of love it or leave it.

How did Briony know what your politics were? I can't imagine new lovers talking politics.

Lovers live in each other's minds. Briony found in mine a degree of civic intensity that she recognized from her father's conversation. Except I was of a different era.

I see.

You don't know everything about me, Doc, you're only hearing what I choose to tell you. I've always responded to the history of my times. I've always attended to the context of my life.

The context.

Yes, as it ripples in concentric circles all the way out to the stars. Bill was a bright little man and I did honor Briony's request, though it wouldn't have occurred to me in any case as a guest in this house to tease out our political differences. But between Bill and me, I would say I was the truer patriot. If you keep the larger picture in mind you can't be convinced of the permanence of this country. Not when you know who's running it.

As you do?

Oh, yes! As I know myself.

Bill and Betty were not disproportioned dwarves, with large heads or torsos, and short legs, they were perfectly proportioned, everything in harmony with everything else. They lived on what I assumed was a fixed income and took pains to live meticulously and with dignity. Bill was show-business handsome, his small fine features and pale blue eyes obviously the source of Briony's good looks. He was somewhat florid, with a head of white hair neatly pompadoured. Betty had the flat doll-like face more often seen in Diminutives. They dressed as Southern Californians, in light colors, crisp slacks, shirts and blouses, penny loafers for him, open flats for her. Betty was a bit stout of figure, but with her dyed brown hair done up in a short bob, and a lovely smile and a face whose default expression was sympathetic understanding. With their outgoing personalities they did emanate the show-business life they had lived. They had toured with various troupes of performing midgets, singing, dancing, or serving in World's Fair tableaus in the native costumes appropriate to various foreign pavilions. They told me all about it. They had played Las Vegas. An entire wall in Bill's study was covered with photographs— inscribed headshots of entertainers I'd never heard of. They'd done some television, toured with Ringling Bros., there were pictures of Betty standing on a cantering horse, of Bill dressed as a drum major and leading a band of clowns. But never sideshows, Bill said, it never came to that and if it did we still wouldn't.

Tell me, Doc, why do things in miniature bring out our affection? Like those little metal cars we all played with as kids that were models of real cars. How important to us that they were accurate to scale. And what about cats, I never liked cats but I could play happily with a kitten, testing its reflexes with a piece of string. And here were Bill and Betty. Toy people, kitten people, accurate to scale. The idea of them was alluring, each moment in their presence was as original as the moment before. It was as if you had traveled to another land, some exotic place on earth that you could write home about, if you had a home and someone there to write to. Not everyone can hope for the experience of being made welcome by these people and treated as an equal, as it were, as if that weren't in itself funny.

So your affection was that of a superior, a taller, grander version of humanity.

Not necessarily. After a few days they were the norm. With the four of us at the dinner table, Briony seemed huge in my eyes, she wore a dress for dinner and had her hair combed back and reaching almost to her shoulders. She was this lovely but ungainly Alice in Wonderland. Me, I was under the illusion that if I stood up too suddenly I'd bang my head on the ceiling. And their voices, Bill's and Betty's, lacking timbre, something like trumpets played with mutes, were sometimes difficult to hear, as if they were communicating from a great distance.

When one morning Briony and her mother went off in a taxi to shop at a mall, Bill sat me down in their little backyard garden for our morning coffee, lit himself a cigar, crossed his little legs, waited for me to speak of something so that he could tell me what he knew about it. There was an assertiveness to him, some inner demand that he prove himself to whatever person of normal stature he happened to be with. He was a kind of pouncing conversationalist. When I mentioned that Briony and I had been reading Mark Twain aloud, he shook his head and said, What do you think of the ending of *Huckleberry Finn,* Professor? It's a goddamn disaster, isn't it? Ruined the whole story for me. When Tom makes his late entrance, it's Twain throwin' in the towel, coming in with his trickster shtick to wrap things up and while he's at it to make the whole grand thing of Huck and Jim going down the river neither here nor there. I know a little bit about the cruelties of life and I'll tell you, this is a damn shame of an ending, Twain bein' in such a hurry to finish his tale any which way and so crap up what might have been a huge story for all time.

Did you know, Bill, that he stopped work on that book for seven years before coming up with the ending?

Sure I knew, that's what I'm sayin'. Couldn't work it out, and said, Damn it all, I'll just get this thing off my desk. Some more coffee?

Actually, Andrew, I happen to agree with that criticism.

I asked about *The Wizard of Oz*—had he ever worked

maybe not in the movie, that was an earlier generation, but in some stage version? He took a big hit on his cigar and set it down in the ashtray. Professor, never mind the movie, you got to read the book. You haven't, have you?

Got me there, Bill.

According to some, the whole thing is communist.

What is?

The Wonderful Wizard of Oz. See, what the moral is, is don't rely on me, don't trust me, my rule is a scam, you've got the stuff to run things yoursels. You and your comrades. All you got to do to take over is get up your courage, use your brain, everone's your equal, 'cept for some at the top, of course, and the world's your oyster. That's communist allegory, according to some.

I don't know, Bill. An allegory—doesn't that mean everything in it stands for something else? Then who are the Munchkins, and why the Wicked Witch of the West, and why is the road of yellow brick? They would have to stand for something besides themselves.

The yellow brick road, well, that's the way to the gold. The Wicked Witch, well, she's the West, you see, meaning us, and with all those flying monkeys being her military forces, if you don't do something she will be even worse than the phony Wizard. And I know who the Munchkins stand for. Believe me, I'm the authority on that.

I'll tell you about the party they gave us the night before we left.

There was a party?

Bill and Betty—to announce our engagement. It was a mostly Diminutive crowd. You know the way New York neighborhoods become Greek, Italian, Latino, the way Koreans run the convenience stores, the Muslims drive the taxis? So in the same way this town had its share of little people who made their living in show business. One elderly fellow sat in a chair and was deferred to by the others—he had actually been a Munchkin. Maybe the last of them alive. The liquor flowed, and the decibels were birdlike. Naturally the rug was rolled up and Bill and Betty did one of their vaudeville routines, the old soft shoe, a George M. Cohan number, ". . . for it was Mary, Mary, plain as any name can be . . ." And with such grace and ease, laughing as they accomplished this or that move, Bill at one point essaying some kind of double time step and Betty glancing to heaven. One of their friends had hoisted himself up onto the piano bench to accompany them and sing the lyrics in his mute tenor, and it was so fine, Briony and I the audience they played to, Briony sitting on the floor, beside me, her legs tucked under her, and her face luminous with joy. "But with propriety, society will say 'Marie' . . ." Others stepped up to do their signature routines, a mock lecture here, a poetry declamation there, all of it great fun, and I remember at one point the Diminutive pastor of the local church meeting me at the self-service bar and asking what I would do, if I were president, about the terrible turbulence in the world. I said I'd go to war to stop it, and it was against his better judgment but he laughed.

Sounds as if you were having a good time.

Well, I saw how Briony loved her parents' routine, laughing and clapping for something she must have seen a hundred times. Watching her lifted me into a comparable state of happiness. As if it had arced brain to brain. This was a pure, unreflective, unselfconscious emotion. It had taken me by surprise and was almost too much to bear—happiness. I felt it as something expressed from my heart and squeezing out of my eyes. And I think as we all laughed and applauded at the end of the soft-shoe number I may have sobbed with joy. And I was made fearless in that feeling, it was not tainted by anxiety, I at that moment had no concern that I might trip and fall over one of them and squash him to death.

So that cold clear emotionless pond of silence—

I was rising from it to living and breathing, to great gasping breaths of life. Finding redemption in the loving attentions of this girl.

Afterward, we excused ourselves and she led me to

the dead end of the street. We climbed over the retaining wall where a path through the ground cover led down to the beach. We found ourselves alone on the beach, not in moonlight, there was no moon to be seen, but in the misty dim light of the cities to the north, the light pollution of Los Angeles spreading out over the sea. I had resisted going for a swim in daylight, not wanting to display my concave chest and skinny arms to the world. Briony had of course seen me in the nude, but one's structure in a bedroom at night when the predominant light is one's intellectual presence is not the vulnerable thing that a pale white professor of cognitive science, bony and slightly potbellied, conveys to the world on a public beach. But nothing could stop me now, we kicked off our shoes, dropped our clothes in the sand, and ran into the surf, which was warm and lapping. We swam together in the Pacific sea, and kissed of course, and I felt the smoothness of her, the tautness of her nipples in the briny sea, running my hand between her legs, holding her by the waist, kissing her as we clasped each other as we were rolled over and over together, cupped in the curl of the waves.

When we came out I dried her with my shirt and we dressed and sat there on little thrones I built out of the sand. This was the time of peaceful reflection when I chose to satisfy my curiosity. I had seen on the wall of

Bill's study two framed naturalization certificates. Bill and Betty hadn't been born here.

Pop was born in Czechoslovakia, Briony said. That's the Czech Republic now. Mom is Irish, from Limerick.

Well, how did they meet?

Ah, she laughed, then you've never heard of Leo Singer!

At this, Briony jumped up and pulled me to my feet. She walked backward, holding my hands. And she told me about this man who went around Europe finding people like her mom and dad, hiring them and training them to work in his show, Leo Singer's Lilliputians.

Here Briony turned, ran ahead, and found it necessary to do a cartwheel. When she was back on her feet I said, What kind of a show?

Well, Mom says the theme changed every season, and the costumes, but it was essentially vaudeville, with songs and sketches and routines like you saw tonight. Circus acts like jugglers, and wire walkers, people who could play the fiddle behind their back, everything you could think of. The attraction was their size, and how many things they could do anyway that people would come to see and marvel at.

How animated she was telling me this family history—living it, almost, by punctuating her account with handstands, cartwheels, back flips to a standing position, running broad jumps. There on the beach that night to the rhythmic lapping of the surf.

He toured them in all the European capitals and that was how Mom and Dad met. They were in the Leo Singer Lilliputstadt.

So, Doc, did you ever hear of this man, Singer?

No.

That's two of us. But it turns out he was the go-to guy when MGM needed Munchkins for their film. He was this international dealer in Munchkins.

I hear a note of disdain in your voice.

Clearly an operator who infantilized these people, made a spectacle of them, and made himself a fortune in the process.

Didn't you say we all have an affection for what is miniature? And here they were in California, her parents, comfortably retired in their own home, a lovely family.

I know, I know. What was in store for them from their villages if the guy hadn't taken them away? Their parents probably only too relieved. I suppose money changed hands. Bill and Betty must have been young, in their teens or early twenties. And he gave them a profession, a means of self-respect, whereas back home they would have been forever misfits, tolerated, made fun of, or treated with insulting sympathy. But it all smacks of Europe, you know? This sensibility. At least the Munchkins in the film had a fictive identity, they weren't midgets performing, they were these fantasy creatures made up not to look like themselves. Not Bill and Betty or the other Lilliputians. Don't you think this has Europe written all over it?

I'm not sure what you mean.

I mean serfdom, indentured oppression, and all their damn uniforms and monarchal wars and colonizations and autos-da-fé. Baiting bears, that's what I mean, the European culture of bearbaiting. Freak taunting. Jew killing. That's what I mean.

[*thinking*] She was so happy. So I didn't say anything. Did I tell you I had bought her an engagement ring before we made the trip west?

No.

I did. I was doing all sorts of un-Andrew things. Holding hands in public, being happy. And now, on the beach, clowning around, trying to do my cartwheels, my handstands, and falling and getting up with a mask of sand on my face. How she laughed. And as it happens with new lovers, we were tinder. The passion fired up from anything—laughter, the keenness of the moment. Close your eyes, she said, and I felt her brushing the sand away. And then all at once she pushed me down, and as I lay back she was upon me, mouth on mouth, vehemently yanking my trousers down and then flipping us over so that I lay on top of her. When had she pulled up her shift to bare herself? And then the three little words: Put it in, she said. Put it in!

You needn't go into details, Andrew.

It may begin as devotional, your lovemaking, but the brain goes dark, as a city blacks out, and some antediluvian pre-brain kicks in that all it knows to do is move the hips. It is surely some built-in command from the Paleozoic Era and may be the basis of all drumming.

Drumming?

What I mean to say is you're not at your most observant at these times. As if what remaining human mind you have, whatever dim consciousness, has located itself somewhere in the depths of your testicular being. That's why I didn't hear its engine and why I did not immediately understand why the beach seemed to be flying away in the sandstorm around us. But then I looked into her eyes: They were blinded white in terror—of me, or of the unnatural blazing light above us? I have wondered about this ever since—surely it was the searchlight, the whoop whoop air-scything of the helicopter rotors. But given what was later to happen, I've never been able to convince myself that it wasn't in terror of me, of the emblazoned Paleozoan she had lain down with. But in any event I knew instantly that the situation was antithetical. I held my hand over her face, hiding her from them, keeping her hidden with my body, while with my other hand

I essayed to pull my trousers up. Perhaps you know about the beaches at night, in Southern California, how they were patrolled.

I think I may have heard something of the sort.

Yes. And the loudspeaker coming over the roar of the rotors—you cannot believe how low they had settled in the sky just above us—the operators of this black buglike monster, punishing us with flying sand, hovering over us as we scampered to our feet and ran, I holding my shirt over her head, and they keeping us in their beam, accusing us of unspecified but monstrous misdemeanor, of blaspheming civilized life, of contaminating a precious sanctuary of innocent children and players of volleyball.

And then the light went out and the damn thing swooped up and away, kicking sand in our faces as we stood there with our arms shielding our eyes. A few moments later it was as if nothing had happened, the night was quiet, and then Briony laughed and she looked at me and laughed some more, shaking the sand out of her hair and tossing her head, dealing with humiliation as women particularly learn to do, with resigned laughter and a kind of shrug and comic raising of the palms.

We had run all the way to the end of the beach where there was a jetty of piled stone, and in a hollow at the land end of the jetty bodiless eyes in multiple array glowed out from the darkness. Briony said it was a clutch

of feral cats who'd lived here as far back as she could remember. They skulked and hissed. We had come too
close and the hiss enveloped us like the spun web of a
spider. Maybe that was when I began thinking once more
about something besides myself.

Like what?

Like this country of eternal sun and midget popula-
tions and sky police.

The next morning, when we were about to leave, I was
standing out by the car and saying goodbye and Betty
was holding my hands, gently bobbing them up and
down as indication of her fondness. We're so happy she
has found you, Andrew. We want everything for our girl.
We love her beyond words. She is the triumph of our life.

I admit I was hoping these were Briony's adoptive
parents. Why do you suppose that was? I was still recov-
ering from the night on the beach, and standing now
under the oppressive sun I had a sick feeling trying to
accommodate the bizarre facts of my true love's life.
These were her founding circumstances, they marked
her, they were hers, she had been made from them, and
what I had made of her before now—my glorious student in the long sunlit frock and running shoes—had
been incomplete if not illusory. Yes, she was, in the great

American tradition, working her way through college—a financial aid package here, a bank loan there—obviously Bill and Betty were not of much help and so Briony was truly out of the nest, her own person. But I didn't want her to have grown up in this household, in this town, among these people, and walking out of the front door every day of her girlhood to see this unchanging street of the little stucco homes and seashelled flower pots in the little front yards, and with the pale paved streets with no shadows. Everything so clearly the life to bake away a functioning brain. I imagined her as a child going down to that beach and playing in the sand, and picking shells at the water's edge, day after day, year after year. It was the shameful feeling of just a moment, before I drove it from my mind—that all this of California was a fraud. Briony came out the door with her backpack and smiled, gorgeous as ever, and I felt that somehow I had been taken in.

Well, I'm reassured. For a while there, love was making you a dull fellow.

Try to understand. I know it's hard for you, but pretend you are me. This whole thing had been a shock. Wouldn't you feel somehow negated? Was it me she loved, or something about me that was all too familiar to her? Had she intuited it the first day of class when I was writing my name on the blackboard and the chalk broke in my hand and I knocked my books off the lectern? She had picked up everything and smiled with understanding. Grown in this endless sun, amid these awful flowers, her parents, face it, freaks of nature, she'd been nurtured to the weird, the unnatural. It was what she knew, her normal social reality. So who would she find for herself, whom would she be morbidly attracted to, but someone as adorable as a freakishly depressive cognitive scientist klutz, whom she was soon enough comforting after the nihilistic despair of his lectures?

I hear self-loathing.

You do?

Another version of your unworthiness as the lover of this girl. First there was Andrew the anachronism on the football campus, and now the opposite, the all too appropriate proto freak fitting right in.

I said this was the feeling for a moment. We have momentary feelings that don't turn into action, don't we?

We do.

You don't think I'd be stupid enough to give up the love of my life because of some momentary suspicion that was actually a ritual self-denigration do you?

I guess not.

She had gotten away, hadn't she, and now as we drove off, her parents waving from their front door, she wept. It was as if she'd said goodbye to them for the last time. I suppose I was responsible.

Why?

With me there she couldn't pretend anymore that she hadn't grown away from them. She could love them, be grateful to them, but not deny that they were from a world no longer her own.

What had you done?

I had met them.

Briony was a superb athlete but without the sinew, the female musculature. She was a slim slip of a thing. Her limbs were firm and shapely but not tightly knotted, as even a dancer's are. So that all this physical life seemed to me not natural, given her build, but more in the nature of a determination, a self-invoked discipline. So where it came from, why she had found it necessary to top a pyramid of cheerleaders, flip herself around on the high bar, run, jump, train for a purpose other than an intensely physical joy of being, I doubt if she even knew. When she had the baby she did her jogging while pushing the carriage. [*thinking*]

Yes?

Only one time did her determined athleticism fail her. Back in the shadow of the mountains. To show her I was not totally foreign to sports I bought us a couple of tennis racquets and we went over to the college courts to hit. I had played a bit at Yale—not *for* Yale, *at* Yale. I never took any lessons but I somehow knew what was involved and in my loose-limbed ambling way I could run around and get to the ball, I had a pretty good forehand and a less reliable backhand, I could hit a topspin lob and I had a nice drop shot if I needed it. The game was new to Briony, but when I offered instruction, how to grip the racquet, how to position your body to hit a forehand, a backhand, and so on, she wasn't interested. She thought she could get the hang of things by herself. When she couldn't—overhitting, knocking the ball over the fence, or netting it, or missing the ball completely, running frantically this way and that—though I tried always to hit where she could hit it back—she finally lost her temper, slammed the racquet down, and walked off the court, sulking. It was the first time in our life together that I saw her lose her composure.

There were others?

Carrying the baby. I forget what month. She was staining, and that frightened her. She was biting on her knuckles as I called the doctor. It turned out to be nothing. But that one time on the tennis court—I've since wondered if, to show off, I hit some shots I knew she couldn't get to.

[*thinking*]

I've never told you about my time in the army. When I was in the army, at the end of basic training there were nighttime maneuvers. I fell asleep in my foxhole while I was supposed to be guarding the perimeter. A cadre officer woke me up. I was given a hundred push-ups with an M1 on my back, but my platoon sergeant, who was responsible for me, was RA, Regular Army, and he lost his stripes. He was two months from retirement. [*thinking*] I was once at an academic cocktail party expressing myself effusively in this crowded room, flinging my arms out to make some point or other. The back of my hand slammed into the jaw of a woman professor standing off to the right of me. She screamed and sank to the floor. All conversation stopped. I ran to the host's kitchen, and was feeling around in the refrigerator freezer for some ice, lifting aside and holding a couple of liters of vodka. The woman's husband had come after me, shouting, and when I turned I was so startled that I dropped the vodka bottles and broke his foot. In the space of a minute I had taken out an entire family. [*thinking*] I was an undergraduate biology major at Yale. One day in the lab we were doing an experiment with sea anemones—

Andrew, stop.

What? Stop what?

III

I CAN TELL YOU: Last weekend Andrew decided to see his child.

Really!

As you know I've been holding back, holding back, and the fact that you've never brought up the subject, never once urging me to go see her or even asking oh so casually if it had ever occurred to me—

This is something you had to come to out of yourself, your own thinking, your own feeling.

Fine.

After all, you've never even told me her name.

Willa. Her name is Willa. I had left her birth certificate with Martha so there would be no mistake about that. Briony chose the name to honor her father. It's lovely, isn't it? Willa.

Quite lovely.

But think of the difficulties. What would I say? Why would I have come, for what purpose? I didn't know. Did I want her back? And if I did, would that be best for her? And if she was with me, would Andrew the Pretender kick in and somehow put her in harm's way? His child?

And if he had just come for a visit, what would she think, could she relate to him in any way, think of him as her father who hadn't seen her since she was an infant in a car seat? A man who would say Hi and leave again? To say nothing of Martha, who was as likely as not to slam the door in my face.

There are certain legalities it seems to me you could rely on. I'm not a lawyer, but the blood relation always prevails. Parenthood rules unless it can be proven that you're not fit. A drunkard, a homeless man, a criminal, that sort of thing.

That sort of thing?

You just don't give children away in this country as if we were back in the medieval world. When you left Willa, was there anything written? Did you consult a lawyer, sign anything, you and Martha?

I was in despair. I needed help. I had considered suicide.

Oh? That's new.

I was at the point where I talked to Briony as if she was alive. Taking her instructions—how to heat the formula, I would read these things but ask her if I had understood them correctly. She would tell me. Put the little thing over your shoulder to burp her after feeding. She will need something warmer for the coming winter. And when it's time for her shots, off to the pediatrician she goes. She'd laugh, my Briony, to see me in my domesticity, I'd have hallucinations where she'd appear beside me, as in life, and then a moment later be a tiny figure doing cartwheels and handstands and somersaults on the kitchen table. Oh, God. And you want me to consult a lawyer?

You didn't hire anyone to help you?

I had no help, I couldn't think of hiring anyone, I had Briony. I took a leave of absence from my job—an unpaid paternity leave. And then the madness dissolved, and I did go to get help. I was desperate for help. I went to Martha.

Actually it was an impulsive decision on Andrew's part, coming upon him as a kind of blown fuse of the endless thinking as to whether or not he should see his child. He was in his study reading yet another paper theorizing on how the brain becomes the mind. Here the proposition was offered that a brain-emulating artifact might someday be constructed whose neural activity could produce consciousness. This assertion, coming not from a pulp science fiction story of the kind he had read as a teenager but from an esteemed neuroscientist in a professional journal, so startled Andrew that he snapped back in his chair as if from an electric shock, and realized that his radio was tuned to the Saturday afternoon broadcast of the Metropolitan Opera. He now listened and understood that the Boris, of *Boris Godunov,* was dying. The czar calling out, singing out his lament, his prayer, and at last dying with the whispered word in Russian that sounded like *rascheechev, ras-chee-chev,* and then the thump indicating that he had hit the stage of the Metropolitan Opera House. Then this beautifully plaintive leitmotif to indicate yes, Boris the czar was kaput.

Later, Andrew didn't remember if he heard the bells of Moscow in celebration of the tyrant's death, because he was out of there, slipping into his jacket as he ran and catching a cab to Union Station and getting on a Metroliner.

In New York, he walked crosstown to Grand Central and in a shop there bought a toy animal for his Willa, a funny, eye-rolling mechanical puppy who could be wound up and set down to wobble along on his little legs. He thought an animal was the safest thing to give his daughter, who would be three years old by now. Any child from one to ten would enjoy a toy animal.

You see, Doc, it all came back to me in a rush—Martha's house, Martha's large husband—not that I thought he was the Boris who had died that afternoon—I had the impression that he was no longer top-drawer in the opera world—but the house, the scene, Martha walking up the staircase with my baby in her arms. It was as if not a moment had passed and I was still at their front door rubbing the snow from my glasses. And as the commuter train rocked its way to New Rochelle I was no longer afraid how my visit would turn out, no longer adrift in indecision, creating ominous scenarios in my mind. I was going to see my daughter! I felt love for Martha and for Martha's husband, I was overflowing with gratitude to these people who had taken my baby with Briony under their wing. And I found I was even happy with the rickety train ride.

You're going to tell me this didn't end well.

Of course.

When Andrew arrived at Martha's house he knew immediately something was wrong. The snow had been cleared from all the other driveways and front walks on her street, but Martha's property had not been touched. Andrew paid the cabbie and stood with his feet in six inches of snow. The thing about Martha, one of the definitive things, was her impeccable home management. If something didn't work, no matter how incidental, she must have it fixed instantly. She brought forth gardeners, plumbers, electricians, carpenters, painters, roofers, tilers, cleaners, glaziers, and repairmen with esoteric specialties. She tended with solemnity to such details as brass door keyhole covers. It was now eight in the evening of a grim November day. Lights were on in the neighborhood, but the house in front of him was dimly lit as if some sort of séance was going on. I don't know why Andrew thought that. He trudged up the path to the front door and found it ajar. [*thinking*]

Yes, go on.

He called me The Pretender.

Who?

Martha's large husband. That was his greeting. Ah, he said, here's The Pretender. That was the name he'd devised for me when we'd had that drink the day I brought the baby to their door. That I only pretended to be a nice human being generously disposed to my fellow man when in fact I was a dangerously fake person, congenitally insincere and a killer—that's how he characterized me. Andrew the Pretender. And, as I told you, he was not far from the truth. But now when he called me The Pretender I realized whose portrait was up there over the mantel of the living room. It was Martha's husband in his greatest role when he was still active—Boris Godunov. Now, you of course know the story of Boris Godunov.

I'm ashamed to say—

Boris is a kind of Russian Richard the Third. Kills

the rightful heir to the throne, the czarevich Dmitry. Slits the kid's throat and declares himself czar. Thereafter, he's tormented by what he has done. Post-traumatic stress disorder.

OK.

So the years pass and an opportunistic monk, Grigoriy, seeing that he's about the same age as the dead czarevich would have been, goes off to put together an army on the Polish-Lithuanian border. He will advance on Moscow announcing himself as the czarevich Dmitry, the rightful heir to the throne. Boris Godunov is assured that the man is a pretender—that the real czarevich is still dead. But afflicted with guilt, and riddled with religious superstition, Boris can't convince himself that this is so, and he dies. That's the story.

Interesting, but why—

Except for some Holy Fool at court who is heard lamenting Russia's fate as the curtain comes down. Lots of Holy Fools in Russia in those days. You get Fools in Shakespeare too but they're not particularly holy. A Russian Fool is automatically holy. He was drunk, of course.

The Fool?

Martha's large husband. Sprawled in an armchair in full czarist regalia, dethroned as Boris Godunov, dethroned as Martha's husband. Because I knew she wasn't there, not with the house in this condition. Not with him in this condition. I didn't know opera singers owned their costumes—they don't, do they? Yet there he was in that heavy tapestry robe and that knitted crown they affected with the jeweled trimming and the little cross on top. He lifted his glass: To The Pretender, he said, looking at me, and then because he hiccupped his arm jerked back and the contents of his glass made a lovely arc through the air and hit his portrait on the wall behind him, splashing over his face made up as Boris Godunov so that the painting seemed to be shedding tears.

Did this really happen?

What?

Your impulsively going to New Rochelle because you'd heard *Boris Godunov* on the radio and then finding this czarist simulacrum lying around drunk?

I'm not angry at you for asking that question because I hardly believed it myself standing there in that dark living room, which incidentally was unheated, which may have been the reason Martha's large husband had put on that heavy regalia complete with that watch cap of a crown. And, after all, might he not have been listening with some bitterness to the same Saturday broadcast? I stood over him as he looked at me with bleary half-focused eyes. He had lost weight and was no longer the intimidating figure he'd been. He'd been a big humpy manatee of a man, huge and sleek. No more. The double chin, the wide face, the big head, it was all thinned out now, the physiognomy, with his jawline like a wishbone and the hollow cheeks with eyes staring up at me that belonged to a very sick man. I found myself furious, totally unsympathetic, and spoke to him as one speaks to a drunk.

Where is she, where's Martha, goddamn you, where's my child?

He staggered to his feet and began to sing the dying scene in his raspy bass, holding his arms out to me.

I ran upstairs, looked in all the rooms. An empty crib, open empty drawers, empty closet. In the master bedroom a rumpled bed, one closet with just the hangers hanging there. On the floor, some scraps of paper. A folded-up bus schedule. *Ras-chee-chev. Ras-chee-chev.* [*thinking*] Listen, I want to correct the wrong impression I may have given you about my feelings for Briony.

Wait a minute—what did you do then?

What?

After you found Martha gone.

I caught the last train back to Washington. That poor drunk had no more idea where she was than I did. He couldn't even tell me how long she'd been gone. I had the feeling looking around that it had been a while. Of course the kid would be safe with her. She'd left her piano. It was still there in the study. That meant to me Willa was now her life. But there was no rush, this was not an emergency, if I hadn't impulsively taken that trip I would really have been in the dark. So relatively speaking I was up on things.

And there was a little bit of relief there too, do you suppose?

Well, why not? I'm not ashamed to say it. What is more daunting than a judgment in the eyes of a child? It would come eventually, inevitably. It just wouldn't be now. But I was trying to tell you something.

Yes?

See, the door was open and there I stood. So to a man, an opera singer costumed as Boris, and seriously drunk, singing the role there in his living room—what could be more reasonable than for Boris to see the fellow standing at the door as the Pretender Grigoriy, with his Polish-Lithuanian army, arrived to take the crown. I had thought he was talking about me, and maybe he was but somehow now also putting me in the opera. I was the false claimant to the throne, you see?

Was he that drunk?

Drunk or not, he was in the play, casting me as the enemy. Some basis for that in my being Martha's ex. And yes he found just the term, plucked it out of Russian operatic history maybe by way of a deeper recognition. At the root, Andrew is The Pretender, OK? Is that what you want to hear? You've interrupted my train of thought. You guys aren't supposed to do that.

But this is important, don't you think? Didn't he make you mad?

Listen, he knew I did cog science. He was not unintelligent. When I left he was singing his heart out to me, following me to the door. So don't jump to conclusions. I felt sorry for him, to tell you the truth. He kissed me on the top of my head. And then he got down on his knees and begged for my blessing. That's what Boris does in the opera, he begs for the blessing of the Holy Fool who stands in his mind for all of Russia. So I was no longer the Pretender to the throne. I had been recast as the Holy Fool. Or he might have been acknowledging me as one Pretender to another. After all he couldn't exclude himself pretending to be the rightful czar. You weren't there. We were brothers under the skin.

So it was a reprieve, is that what you're saying? You were absolved of being Andrew the Pretender?

We're all Pretenders, Doctor, even you. Especially you. Why are you smiling? Pretending is the brain's work. It's what it does. The brain can even pretend not to be itself.

Oh? What can it pretend to be, just by way of example?

Well, for the longest time, and until just recently, the soul.

I may have given you the wrong impression about my feelings for Briony. But for that moment in California as we left her parents' house, and perhaps a few others, my love was as pure and uncomplicated as never before in any attachment I had had to a woman. I haven't told you about my relationships, some of them seemingly strong. But never uncomplicated.

Before your marriage to Martha?

And after. Trouble with all of them is that I was always myself. With Briony I was the person I'd always dreamt of being. For a person congenitally unable to be happy, I was, with Briony, happy. Happiness consists of living in the dailyness of life and not knowing how happy you are. True happiness comes of not knowing you're happy, it's an animal serenity, something between contentment and joy, a steadiness of the belonged self in the world. Of course I'm talking about life in the developed Western world. A modest busyness in the routine of life, a satisfaction with your lot, the deliciousness of sex and food and fine weather. You don't just love the person you love, you love the given world. A feeling possibly induced by endomorphin, the brain's opiate. I know, there it is again, the cephalic instruction. But so what! As we crossed the country there were snow mountains for the skiers, white-water runs for the rafters, free rides everywhere you looked. We drove one day along a field where in the distance balloonists had convened. We pulled over to watch this languid flotilla of rainbowed sky ships risen into their own blithe sense of time and space. We discussed the possibility that Americans more than any other people understand what the earth and sky have to offer. At these moments life was what it was and nothing more, it was exactly what it seemed to be with nothing behind it. A presiding belief in the future, all the synapses afire as if to make a metaphysical music and you are blissfully existing in the consciousness of the customary given world as the only reality. And of course the guilt is gone. The fear that was your old self. All that, I say, is what Briony did for me. My delight in everything everywhere on that trip was essentially the joy of being with her, the fact that she was with me—everything about her— her thoughtfulness, how she confronted you with her eyes, her laugh, the simplicity of her self-attentions—she wasn't much for makeup, never primped, her hair was brushed, sometimes tied behind the neck, sometimes not. Just by the way she casually fixed her hair she suggested the different aspects of her being. When we fell silent during a stretch of straight road that went on for miles, she sat with her arms crossed, or looked for music on the radio. She was in charge of the music and decided I had a lot to learn, which was true, I'd never gotten beyond the Beatles and the Grateful Dead. (Oh, she said, you mean The Dead.) I wasn't afraid for her, she would never be a victim of The Pretender. I was through with him. I was transmogrified, I was on my way to Holy Fooldom.

But as I say, we were riding across the country and I was the new Andrew, no longer anxious, no longer worried for her. Everything was amazing. Escarpments of red rock, endless fields of wheat, towns of one dusty street, a roadside diner where you moved down along a steam table and took what you liked to the cashier, a sign on the wall announcing: "Efficient and Courteous Self Service." A trailer park in a sandstorm, the wind whipping up the clotheslines, a motel with a purple dinosaur on its roof, seemingly endless wooden one-room Baptist churches with the day's chapter and verse out front, antebellum towns with pillared mansions shadowed in live oak. In Atlanta we stopped at a bookstore and bought a bunch of Mark Twains, and on the interstate whoever was not driving read him aloud—we took turns—Briony drove well, not impatiently but not dillydallying either. I saw Mark Twain in her eyes as we passed under the repetitive amber lights of the highway, and I saw him flickering in her imagination—

So, there was your MT. *Huckleberry Finn,* I suppose?

The Prince and the Pauper. The two boys exchange identities, the prince is the pauper and the pauper the prince. Briony liked the romance of that, Clemens saying there's nothing to royalty but the assumption. But it's more than a democratic parable: It's a tale for brain scientists. Given the inspiration, anyone can step into an identity because the brain is deft, it can file itself away in an instant. It may be stamped with selfhood, but let the neurons start firing and Bob's-your-uncle.

I'm not sure of the timing of your trip. Had Briony graduated? I thought you said she was a junior when you met. Were you reappointed for a second year?

I remember coming up the Jersey Turnpike, past the oil refinery burn-offs, and with the growling of the convoying semis in our ears, and away off to the left the planes dropping to the runways of Newark Airport and then the fields of burned grass irrigated by rivulets of muck and with what looked like a buzzard floating over the turnpike risen now on concrete pillars that in their tonnage were holding up the furious intentions of traffic, the white lights coming toward us, the red lights beckoning, and when I glanced over at Briony she was staring straight ahead, clearly stunned by this dazzling information, it wasn't exactly fear in her eyes but more like a virginal response to the unexpected. What I wondered at that moment was how much time one got for transporting a young woman across state lines. What is it you asked?

When this was, and did she drop out of school to go with you.

Briony was half junior, half senior, when I came along. She was graduated in January, when there was no commencement. She had her various jobs while I rode out my year's contract. With Briony sometimes auditing in her front-row seat I was inspired to give the students only good news: how much neuroscience is advancing almost day by day. I was positive, always anticipating a resolved future of essential discoveries, it was the guarded optimism of the classroom, the assumption of any science course, that we would get to the truth eventually. I harked back to Whitman, who knew better than anybody what we are and sang of "the body electric." How pleasing to those children to learn, body as brain and brain as body, that it all came together. Of course I wouldn't tell them he was a poet. Ruin everything.

So there we were. I had taken her out of her organized life, removed her from her horizontal bar, and moved us to New York. In fact, she loved the city. We found a place after a while in the West Village. An apartment in a converted warehouse, with a loading-dock entrance and iron front windows, a creaky elevator, old unpolished wooden floors. Three rooms, lots of light, trees on the block, wonderful stores in the neighborhood, and of course the storekeepers all got to know Briony, the Italian bakery on the corner with the fresh breads in the window, the Korean food market, the coffee shop, newsstand. Because she was lovely, outgoing, cheerful, friendly, asking questions, warming up all these crotchety New Yorkers, who responded, to their own amazement, in kind. Andrew, she said, everything you need is right here, you don't have to drive to a mall to shop, when was this invented! And we would walk everywhere, she wanted to explore, we walked to Chinatown, we walked over to Washington Square, where I had lived as a child, she got to know the city quite well.

How did you live?

I had a contract from a textbook publisher to do a kind of cog sci workbook. And then for the same company I became an outsource editor for their science lists. Reading books and proposals. And Briony tutored in math. She put something on the Internet and in no time at all she had more clients than she wanted—high school kids, middle school kids—testament to the state of education in America. So we made out OK. This was before the baby, you understand. When the baby came, a cake was delivered by the old Italian baker, the Koreans sent over a basket of fruit, all the old ladies of the neighborhood had tracked her pregnancy, she was everyone's expectant young mother, and when on a spring day Briony brought Willa out for the first time, carrying her in a chest sling, somehow people appeared, it was as if they had been waiting, it was a kind of royal procession, Mother and Child, Briony couldn't walk ten feet without someone stopping to ooh and aah.

What about you?

Well, I was there, of course, hanging in the background. I had never connected with the neighbors as Briony had. I just kept a smile frozen on my face, saying nothing and being more or less ignored. But I'll tell you how lovely it was to watch Briony nurse our little girl, her cheeks flushed with happiness, her eyes on the baby and then on me with an expression of such fruition, as to enunciate in that moment the magnificence of life. And it was all in her eyes, my dear wife of twenty-two, who had the strength of being to totally transform me, turn me into something resembling a normal, functioning citizen of the world. [*thinking*] Ach, God.

Kleenex on the little table there.

So now you know why I'm here.

I do.

It's a kind of jail, the brain's mind. We've got these mysterious three-pound brains and they jail us.

Is that where you are?

I've known it for some time. I'm in solitary, one hour in the yard for the exercise of memory. You're a government psychiatrist, aren't you?

Well, I'm board-certified, if that's what you mean.

And I thought we were travelers on the road together. The two of us, walking down the road. On the other hand I don't think you travel well. I suppose you've never been to Zagreb.

Zagreb?

I was in a park there where every little bush and sprig of flowers was identified with a card on a metal stand. You had to bend down to read the Latin name. I was there with the woman who did the all-in-the-air somersault.

I see.

She was a prostitute, of course. And why I said to the pimp that her act was too brief to hold an audience for an entire evening, I don't know. Perhaps I was drunk. Perhaps the somersault only seemed to be entirely in the air. She was a soft-spoken little woman habituated to submission. She smiled through her tears as she asked me to take her away from Zagreb, there in the park on a chilly autumn afternoon with the little bushes labeled carefully as if this was a truly civilized part of the world that had never seen war and whose native population didn't hate the Serbs or the Bosnians, and who hadn't made themselves into a puppet state of the Nazis in World War II. I saw this sedate, meticulously botanized park with the autumn leaves blowing across our path as a claim in the name of civilization to deny the brutal history of this place.

What were you doing there?

Just wandering. I had set off across Europe, hitchhiking with some other Yalies, but one by one we went our separate ways and there I was in Zagreb. In the hotel an old man in a tuxedo played the piano. American songs from years before as if they were the latest numbers. "My Blue Heaven." "How High the Moon." "Mr. Sandman." And in a stiff clumsy unsyncopated way that revealed his obdurate classical training. Even Martha could do a proper swing tune if she was in the mood. I was the only American in the place, so I guess the performance was for me. A dark little room with red draperies and stuffed chairs and ottomans with the shape of buttocks worn into them. Just a few customers sitting in attitudes of waiting with their drinks untouched in shot glasses. The waiter nodding off in a corner. They all seemed in cahoots, the big bulky pimp, the pianist, and the customers—all of them there to demonstrate that this was the place to be, this third-rate hotel in this sadly unremarkable city of interest not even to the people who lived there. And she wasn't the only one, the somersaultist . . .

The only one what?

Who asked me to take her away.

So this was not a dream.

There was a woman in St. Petersburg who asked the same thing. I don't remember how I met her. Maybe at the Hermitage. She wore white stockings, a cherubic girl with her stockings held up by her generous thighs. Whose white-stockinged legs pointed skyward with almost military precision and then separated, widening like calipers.

Why are you telling me this?

Because I remember it. Because I don't want to speak of what happened. It was clear wherever I went that I had no money. A student with a backpack, skinny and perpetually anxious. Yet this is what people do, when they are driven to it. With my American passport I was a commodity. Why are you looking at me like that? I'm trying to tell you that before I married Martha I had my share of adventures with the race of women.

I see.

With one marriage and several affairs behind me I

was under no illusions. So that I did not impute to Briony her moral beauty, her natural unschooled virtue. It was really there. Nothing about her was practiced except perhaps her acrobatics. She came to me as Revelation. Not only because of the death of Martha's and my baby girl, but because as a youth, as a student, I had been stupidly, cockily uncaring, not yet cunningly the resolved accidental killer-pretender but merely a heedless sort of lout like some of my collegiate pals.

I see.

There was one extended affair at Yale. I refused to marry her. So it ended as it had to at graduation and she went off to Spain, I think it was, with her degree in comparative lit, a tall pretty girl with dark eyes, and not long after there in the mail were her wedding pictures. The groom was not only a cognitive scientist, he even looked like me. So that when she wrote a few years later to tell me that she was leaving him I knew it was all over between us. You're smiling.

I am.

But it wasn't funny. We were very intense, it was something we'd gotten into and couldn't get out of. She became pregnant in our junior year. We discussed that for a few furtive, dismaying months. But then she miscarried. This happened one evening when I was with her in her rooms. She called to me from the bathroom. The

water in the bowl was plum-colored, and floating huddled with his knees drawn up was my tiny replica. Smaller
than a mouse but unmistakably of family, with my same
domey head and bunched brow in a frown, everything
coming to a point in the chin. Not pleased at all, my heir,
looking inward of course.

IV

I KNOW THAT WHEN women have their babies the husband takes second place, it's to be expected that the mother-infant bond prevails and the husband finds himself usurped.

Yes, that sometimes happens.

Well, that did happen in a gentle kind of way with Briony and our baby, that maternal fixity of attention, but it was enough to worry me. What if it was more than that? I noticed that whenever I left things of mine scattered about—newspapers, books—she'd pick them up and put them where she decided they belonged. She had this alarming sense of order. Surely as time went on our different ways would add up. I began to think of the future—how with the passing years the disparity of our ages would become more pronounced. I decided to join a gym and work out.

Not really.

Yes, I entered the world of abs and pecs and quads. No two-syllable words in that crowd. I hated the place, all these heroes with weight lifter belts around their waists, heaving bars loaded with metal plates the size of sewer covers and grunting, and shouting, popping their muscles and then strutting around in display of their magnificence. I couldn't bear it there for more than a few minutes—working this or that machine for fifteen reps—not repetitions, reps, and why fifteen was the sacred number I never did learn. But Briony approved—thought it was a good idea that I perform exercises, get up from my desk and fit myself to those machines. Cheers your brain, don't you know, she said in the closest thing to flippancy that I had ever heard from her. As if I hadn't taught her about the brain-body nexus.

Do you think, Andrew, you may sometimes overreact?

In the nineteenth century, work was physical. Blacksmiths, capenters, hod carriers, farmers, dam builders, ditch diggers, layers of railroad track, slaughterers of cattle. People didn't have to find ways to exercise. Do you know what the New York Marathon is?

Of course.

If I ever were to decide to do serious research in neuroscience—well, it would have to do with the communal brain. As with ants, as with bees.

Why?

The brain of an ant colony is the colony. The brain of a beehive is the hive. And we have our popular delusions and the madness of crowds. Fellow who wrote that knew more than he knew.

You mean the tulip bubble?

Why do schools of fish change direction instantly, as one? Why do flocks of birds, leaderless, fly in changing patterns with more precision than a ballet company? Think of wars. How they become unavoidable and once begun grow bigger and bigger. Or the bizarre indigenous practices of any religious group no matter what god it attests to. And people going to the park on Sunday. Why should the day for the park be Sunday?

Families are together for the day of rest and so on. We have cities and we put parks in them for sound and obvious reasons.

No, Doc, it's only a true park on Sunday, it needs a large amount of people to find its definition as a park, because a park is only a park when it organizes a human colony, and the fact that that is temporary shouldn't blind us to the fact that it is repetitive.

Andrew—

The collective brain is a powerful thing. But we can't compare to the ants, the bees. They have pheromonal cloud brains—chemical instructions for everything— sex, war, foraging. Millions or billions of years from now when the planet is long crisped and the human race is extinct, ants will reign, or maybe fruit flies, or maybe both, and they'll be archaeologically inclined, they will crawl over the ruins of our cities, arrange our bones, display our remnants in museums of natural history, they will fly into the open windows of our skeletal apartments, rise up our elevator shafts, explore our long underground tunnels in their effort to understand who we were and what we were up to with our stacked caves of steel and stone and on the streets and runways our rusted-out prosthetic devices to move us from one place to another.

You're suggesting they will survive us?

The collective brain of the ant colony is outside the body of any individual ant. It is the gaseous chemical identity of a colony that governs every ant's behavior. So that looking at them you might think they know what they're doing. Or why they're doing it. Or it's possible that the colonial brain invests each ant with an intelligence he or she might not otherwise have. That interests me. And the chances of survival are improved exponentially.

I seem to recall your quoting Mark Twain about the stupidity of ants.

That was of a particular ant who'd individualistically wandered off on his own. Nevertheless he, the ant, was capable of carrying three or four times his own weight. I didn't see the equivalent from the grunts lifting sewer covers in my gym.

Why are we having this discussion?

We do pale emulations of the group brain as if in envy. We give ourselves temporarily to a larger social mind and we perform according to its dictates the way individual computers cede their capacities to their network. Perhaps we long for something like the situation these other creatures have—the ants, the bees—where the thinking is outsourced. Cloud thinking, a chemical ubermensch. Which brings us to politics.

I'm not sure you're serious.

You know Emerson? It's what Emerson, thinking of his own kind of creature, mistakenly calls the oversoul. He romanticizes it, makes it a constituent of ethical thinking suggesting God. When all he is aspiring to is a kind of universal pheromonal genius.

Seriously, Andrew, are you planning to do this research?

And then, of course, fashion. Even Briony wore jeans. Even I. And then our slang, the way a phrase will catch fire and go through all of us, all at once indispensable, ubiquitous, until it dies out as quickly as it arose. [*thinking*] What?

Your plans for the future.

Don't make me laugh, Doc. I'm telling you about the end of my life.

We were getting ready to go out. A Sunday morning, a beautiful May morning, and we were to have brunch at this little French place on Sullivan Street. Briony was well into her eighth month and moving somewhat slowly, and while I waited I turned on our new TV I had bought to certify us as a family. And as it happened there was this documentary about the New York City Marathon. And there were the marathoners, in full color, streaming across the Verrazano Bridge by the thousands. For a moment I had the illusion that Briony was among them. But she appeared beside me, materialized as if from the screen.

All thoughts of leaving for our brunch were put aside, so rapt was she.

It is, after all, a remarkable sight, this legion of runners advancing like a tidal wave over the silver bridge, these thousands all doing the same thing at the same time, a great swath of humanity putting itself to the test of running twenty-six or so miles without falling down dead. I have to admit there is something so clean and spare about it, with its ancient allusions. How it exalts people to do this thing that has no reward except for having done it. There are purses, of course, for the world-class long-distance runners who come from other countries to breast the finish line, a man, a woman, gender indistinguishable in their running shorts and their numbered ribbed shirts and running shoes and sinewy bodies, crossing the finish line hours before the masses. [*thinking*] She hadn't known about it, my wife. So it was as if all those runners were about to sweep us up, carry us along, engulf us in the tide of them.

Was this so portentous, people running?

I knew it before she said it, Briony right then and there swearing to run in the coming marathon. With a resolute nod to herself. With a clenching of fists. This was the girl, after all, whom I had seen for the first time spinning around the high bar. I had to smile—here she was, melon-ripe, and planning to begin training like the moment she delivered—but she wasn't joking and was put out with me for not taking her seriously. I want to do this, Andrew, and I will. I don't care what you say. And that's all there is to it.

This wasn't the first time Briony could sound like the willful child who fixes her mind on something and won't listen to reason. Made me think Bill and Betty must every now and then have had their hands full.

She couldn't take her eyes off the screen. And when the camera cut away from the leaders to the main body, people on the sidewalks holding out cups of water and cheering, a runner here limping, a runner there gasping for breath, the strain on some faces, the concentration so that you understood they saw and heard nothing but the pavement in front of them, the robotic pounding of their own feet—well, when I looked at Briony I was chastened to see the tears running down her cheeks. She sat there on the couch leaning forward, as if something religious was going on. And so I wasn't about to argue. When the program was over I hugged her and said not a word about how unrealistic it was there in June to think, the baby coming momentarily, that she could recover quickly enough and turn herself in the few months till November—that's when they have it—into a long-distance runner through five boroughs and twenty-six-some miles over bridges and up hills and down avenues. I said to her only that the baby and I would be waiting for her at the finish line in Central Park.

Willa thoughtfully chose to be born just a few days later. How long was it before Briony was doing her jog those summer mornings with the baby carriage flying before her? Sometimes I took them in a cab to Central Park and sat with the carriage while Briony ran around the reservoir. I would do my reading, holding the baby when she fretted, giving her her bottle—I was fearless. And after a while there would Briony be, gleaming with health, laughing, her arms shining, her shirt stained with sweat, and as she drank from her water bottle, head tilted back, I studied the loveliness of her neck, the peristalsis of her throat. And then right there on the bench in the sun she would unbutton her nursing bra and give the baby her breast, and there were mother and child, a sacrament of nature in the green park among the families drifting by, dogs barking, kids on scooters, the wandering seller of balloons.

You're describing an idyll.

How is it that first mothers instantly have the knowledge of mothering? Something that's always been in the brain is called into play. And the organization. Somehow she found time for everything—the baby, her tutoring, seeing after the old lady who lived next door. Into July and August on the hottest of days she would leave the house at dawn for a serious run and do her miles, seven, ten, by the time people were going off to work. She would head downtown to where the offfice buildings were, and find one where she could run the stairs, run up twenty, thirty flights of stairs for strength training.

I assume you approved all of this.

Of course. Wasn't I working out at the gym? We were a team, including Willa out to see her mother run the marathon. Briony bounded off from our doorway and her feet barely touched the ground. Her legs seemed to grow longer, it was like the levitation you see in classical ballet. [*thinking*]

Yes?

I had also bought us a phone with an answering machine. "Hello, Briony? Bri, are you there? It's Dirk! I got your number from your folks."

Her old boyfriend? The football player?

Briony was out. She was tutoring.

Did you tell her?

Of course I told her. She called back and agreed to meet him for lunch. She told me he'd gotten a job at a brokerage downtown.

No more football?

Said he would never make the pros. He was a business major and his father knew people in New York.

How did you feel about this?

I felt in bed at night that she pressed herself to me as she always had. I felt that our baby that we'd made was in her crib next to the bed. I felt Briony's heartbeat in my chest as my own. Why do you ask these questions—that the love of my life would not be trustworthy, is that what you think? Or that I would think? It was all in her fine honest lovely young face without guile, without secrets, that she had made up her mind, and she had her family now. But they were old friends, and why not? We didn't even talk about it.

So it was no problem.

The day was the problem. It was the day. It was the morning of the day that they were to have lunch that was the problem. [*thinking*] You might say that. She got up later than usual because Willa had had a fretful night. So it was almost eight when she went out for her run. It was to be a busy day. When she had done her miles she'd shower, put on something appropriate for lunch in a restaurant, see that the old woman next door was OK, and after her lunch with Dirk she had two hours of afternoon tutoring. So it was a busy day. [*thinking*] She kissed my cheek: Willa likes the applesauce for her morning snack, she said, and set off over the route she had worked out for herself: down along the Hudson to the Esplanade, across Liberty Street, with maybe a stop at the WTC to run some flights of stairs, and then turning north up Broadway.

"Briony, it's not to be. I have to cancel." Here a laugh becoming a sob. "I wouldn't mind so much if I could see you one last time. But then you'd have to be up here and I wouldn't want that. Wouldn't want that. Or just to talk to you— Are you there, Bri? Hello? Oh, God. It's their machine."

Andrew, what is this?

Giving you Dirk on the answering machine: "Okay, Professor, I'm leaving a message. That's your voice, isn't it? Am in the window frame now. Far as I can go. High altitude. Heat is something. . . . Standing on the bare steel. . . . Isn't it neat that your machine is getting this because it is surely the end of me. So I am finished but everything else will go on including you, especially you, Professor. . . . We don't hear as good as bats, see as well as hawks. You remember saying that? We can know only so much. You remember? So I wanted to ask then, how can you be so fucking sure there's no God? Hear your bullshit answer."

He was that conversational—that he could think of that?

I'm giving you his words. There were pauses when the sound of unimaginable catastrophe took over. Then his voice would return as from a distance. "My understanding of jumping from high places is that I will be dead . . . before I hit the ground. I surely hope so. I surely do hope so. Won't I be like flying? I'll be flying, I'll be in free flight. It will be cool because it's hot as hell here. I think it is time now, steel—*yi!*—melting my shoes. Just step off, why not, why not. I'll put the phone in my pocket and he will hear my flight, and keep it for posterity, deliver it as a lecture: How Bri's lover died. Professor, you old fuck, you stole her from me with your smart-ass talk. But hear me: You make a good life for her, live for her, or I will come back and haunt you. I will inhabit your goddamn brain."

Good lord—

And then I heard the flame behind him like a whoosh of a monstrous breath and think now, as I have listened to the point where I don't have to listen to hear it, I hear too the voices of the others on the ninety-fifth floor with him as they burned to death, their cries the last organic traces of their enflamed bones, a weird awful chorus finally indistinguishable from the roar of the oil fire and the cringe and screech and squeak of the tortured steel and from the oily smoke of flames that refueled from the smoke and blew out again to flame. And then I hear air in its resistance to a falling body, it is like the sound of a jet engine louder and louder in higher and higher pitch and it lasts but a few seconds before it ceases to be sound, before I hear only the absence of sound followed by a beep of the answering machine terminating the call.

So it was that morning.

Yes.

What did you do then?

Nothing.

I don't understand.

Nothing! By the time I came back in and noticed the light blinking it was all over. Christ, Doc, what country were you in that day? Who in the entire city didn't know in a flash what had happened. Where was Briony, where was my wife! I was out in the street holding the baby in my arms and looking for her. Calling her name. Looking for her to turn the corner and appear. In the confusion, the fire engines, people stumbling through the streets, shouting, sirens, it was as if all of that had swallowed her up. Where was she? She would think first of Willa. She'd be back in a second to make sure the baby was all right. Wouldn't she? Then where was she?

Oh, Andrew . . .

Or was she trapped there! I went back to the apartment and found a neighbor who would stay with the baby. And then I ran downtown. Of course I couldn't get near anything. One of the towers had sunken in on itself. People staggered by me to get away, people covered in ash, as if cremated but the form of them not yet collapsed. I thought I saw her. Briony! I stopped her—these eyes looked out at me from a gray mask, bright terrified eyes as the only living part of her, this woman. I actually tried to brush the ash from her face. What are you doing? she said. Get away! It was useless—the lines were up, the stanchions, police, fire, ambulances, lights strobing, the squawking of their radios. I waited at a corner, waiting to see her among the fleeing faces. And then I knew that was hopeless and decided that if I ran home she would be there. . . . But it was just the light flashing on the machine.

Had she instinctively run toward the disaster, leaping into the firestorm, by nature a first responder? I didn't know. Only later, haunting the police stations, was I deranged enough to think it was Dirk she wanted to rescue, to climb ninety-five flights of stairs to pull to safety, catastrophically, insanely, passionately. In my bad moments I thought it was that. But she might not even have known where he worked. They were to have lunch in the neighborhood down there. Anyway, what difference did it make? He broadcast his death, but her silence was what connected them in my mind. It was as if their simultaneous deaths, each unknown to the other, could be construed as a peculiar coalescing of their fates—their transformation into star-crossed lovers. But that is only if I put me in the picture.

I wouldn't do that if I were you.

Nothing recognizably Briony was ever found. [*thinking*] How calmly I have said that.

The neighbors knew because they knew her. They filled the house. They held the baby.

There were in the street these posters everywhere plastered, on every wall, on every fence, on mailboxes, on phone booths and in subway stations, with the photographs of intensely alive, of can't possibly be dead, faces. Name, age, last seen. Phone numbers in black marker. Have you seen this person? Call this number. Please call. I went around putting up the picture of Briony. Name, age, last seen. I wanted people to see her face. I knew it was useless, but I thought it necessary. I had taken it in the park, she was smiling at me. I had a folder with her faces, a hundred copies, printed at a Kinko's, and I went around posting them. She was in that community of the last seen, their names and addresses, that they were loved. Please call. She was in that community of what was left of them.

And beside the firehouses, or against the schoolyard fences, or on signboards under streetlamps, were the makeshift shrines of their pictures, or their children's drawings, nestled in sprays of evergreen and framed by candles and with bunches of flowers, and petals in bowls of water. It took another day or two before I found flowers at our door.

I endured what I could. I couldn't sleep. I lay in bed listening for the key turning in the lock. The women of the neighborhood helped for a couple of weeks. After that I was on my own. Willa would look at me with her mother's blue eyes. Quietly judgmental, I felt, though knowing that could not be true. Fretful at times, looking past me, looking for Briony. I rocked the carriage back and forth. And then in November they held their marathon as a national vow to prevail. It grew colder. Snow fell. And there I was swaddling Willa, pushing the little feet into the leggings, the arms into the sweater, and then the hat and the snowsuit and the blanket and the whole bundle of her into the car seat. It is an arduous process, preparing an infant for the outdoors in winter. And when I had buckled her in and started the engine I realized what I had in mind: I would bring her to Martha.

V

HELLO, DOC, why I'm here on the mountainside overlooking this fjord is to get as far away from you as possible. I am in a cabin with not even the work of MT to pass the time. Not even Knut Hamsun. I have a table, a chair, a cot, a sink, a camp stove, and a toilet. As compact as a prison cell except I can stand in the doorway and see the Norwegian mountains framing the valley of icewater—darker in hue than the Wasatch, green-black they are, more into themselves than the sun-specked Western cousins, humpier, and more sedate. When it rains that's when I have my shower. Regularly a cruise ship, toy-size, floats by down there, soundless from this height but as if to affirm the self-satisfaction of the people who claim these fjords for their national heritage. I can shout and hear my voice coming back a moment or two later, faintly, and maybe only in my imagination. I do that to believe I'm not alone. I sing a lot as well, I remember the words of the old Hit Parade numbers. Without my knowing it, my brain had stored dozens and dozens of lyrics in neuronal connection with the tunes. If I say the words the tune comes to me. Can't have one without the other. I also have a tin mirror over the sink and I look into it so that someone is there beside me. I have done this because Wittgenstein did it. He who understood so well the deceptions of the thinking brain. But it is dangerous to stare into yourself. You pass through endless mirrors of self-estrangement. This too is the brain's cunning, that you are not to know yourself.

I'm writing this though there's no mail here and chances are you won't read it till I get back and hand it to you and sit there watching you read. If I ever do. I understand why you asked those questions in the midst of my living through it again—as I spoke of it and recited the voice machine death message wired into my brain, and then Briony's death message delivered as in a silent film, her face speaking to me earnestly in words I cannot hear, the shutter closing around her face, the aperture contracting to a pinpoint and finally to black . . . because all you could muster was: Had I informed Briony's parents. That was you, ever the practical fellow, tidying things up, expecting people to do what was logical and right. Living by the book. What about Bill and Betty, you said, shouldn't you have called them? Assuming I didn't. In fact they were on the phone almost the moment it happened, with their distant trumpet-mute voices. She's not home yet, I said, but don't worry, I'll have her call you . . . trying to sing through the trembling in my voice.

If I could go mad surely that would be better than the sanity of this meditative solitude. *Me and my shadow . . . Dancing in the dark.* I do have a big bread knife that I look at from time to time. It looks back.

They died soon after. Bill of a stroke, Betty withering away. Tiny coffins for them, a jar of unidentifiable anonymous ash standing in for Briony. The whole family shamed by the facility of their transfiguration.

Do you want this returned?

No, keep it. It was written to you.

In any event I'm glad you're back. I didn't know you were into popular music and liked to sing.

Well, I'm a different man in a fjord.

VI

ANDREW SOLD OFF the furniture, broke his lease, and left New York. The city was Briony's now. He saw her running through the streets, looking back at him, turning a corner. Besides, there was no work to be found. He'd read in *The Chronicle of Higher Education* of a cog science clinical professorship at George Mason University, but the interview did not go well and he knew nothing would come of it. So there he was in Washington, thinking maybe he could run a study on the collective brain of an administration using the model of an ant colony. But the only job to be found was as a substitute science teacher at a D.C. high school. He took it. Within a month, one of the science teachers had a heart attack, and so there was Andrew with the pay of a substitute and the hours of a full-timer. He found himself a studio apartment and settled in as a Washingtonian. It suited his sense of his life as a lost cause to have demoted himself from academia to a public high school.

A lost cause? Can we talk more about this?

I can tell you the high school building was a ruin. Paint peeling everywhere, broken furniture, bathrooms

out of order, cracks like earthquake fissures in the black-
boards, window shades that either wouldn't come down
or wouldn't go up, and the musty atmosphere of dust
and mildew. He established his popularity immediately
by sitting down at his desk in front of a class and slowly
tilting out of sight, his chair, he had not noticed until it
was too late, one with but three legs. Immediately, de-
spite their laughter, several students were beside him,
lifting him to his feet, bringing over a working chair, and
he knew this had not been a trick on their part. In fact,
perhaps because of the woeful condition of the school,
the teachers and students seemed to bond in a fellowship
of the indomitable. The kids tacked their pastel drawings over holes in the walls, they painted their history
murals, worked on their end term musical, cheered their
basketball team. Teachers and students were on a first-
name basis, and everyone had lunch in the same lunch-
room, what had been the separate dining preserve of the
teachers having filled over the years with broken
equipment—projectors, tape recorders, TV sets, filing
cabinets, tables, chairs, an upright piano with half the
keys missing. Andrew was given the lesson plan in biology. It was simple enough and he used the occasion of
the frog dissection, and a reprise of Galvani, the leg of a
dead frog touched with a metal probe twitching as if still
alive, to gradually direct the class to some elementary

facts of brain science. And the more he wandered off the lesson plan, the more they loved it, girls and boys, the inseparable lovers among them. One of the students jumped up on the stage of the study hall and held his fist to his mouth, microphonelike: "Here it's dorsal, there it's ventral, this here's rostral, you nothin' but mental . . ."

But this school was not where you were headed with your coffee and paper the morning a voice asked you to fix the screen door?

No, by then I had an office in a converted cleaning closet in the White House basement.

A cleaning closet in the White House basement.

Yes. I hated to leave those kids. They kept me afloat. They buoyed my spirits. The white mice in the maze I built—they loved that. Watching how a mouse brain learns the world. Oh, and "the two thieves dilemma." Standard first-term cog sci. That really turned them on: Two thieves whom the evidence is not enough to convict are told each in turn and privately by a clever detective that the other has betrayed him and spilled the beans. So each is given a choice. Betray in turn, or keep mum. If they both betray they will both get, say, ten years in prison. If one betrays the other, he will get five years, and the one who doesn't betray will get twenty. If neither of them betrays the other they will both go free. So what is the best strategy for each thief? He has to figure if the other will betray him or not and what he should do in either case. We played that several times with volunteer thieves taking turns standing outside in the hall. The class booed the betrayers, made fun of them. They applauded when the decision not to betray was chosen by both volunteers.

You seemed to have found a home in that high school.

I did have a strong sympathetic connection to the place, to the teaching of children, to being caught up in their exuberant time of life. That surprised me. From eight to three I whited myself out. There was nothing behind me, no memory.

But you chose to leave.

I hadn't been teaching a month when, in the middle of a period, a bunch of people blew unannounced into my classroom, my principal leading. Three or four men in suits with cables winding into their ears, photographers with their cameras, what I took to be a couple of women newspaper reporters. Nobody said anything until the door opened again, a man slipped in and stood there by the door, and then behind him, striding in with a big smile, the president of the United States interrupting my lesson on mind reading.

My goodness. What was the occasion?

No occasion, it was just a photo op, some routine puffery. He wrote his name on the cracked blackboard.

He told the students how proud he was of the way they made the best of things, stayed in school, and were not brought down by the conditions around them. How they were being made strong, tempered like steel, and how cool that was, the implication being that poverty was good for them. The kids were stunned, they didn't even laugh when his chalk broke. He told a few of them to come up and have their picture taken with him. Never has a high school classroom been more thunderously silent. I had been elbowed out of the way to stand by the window. With my back to the sun I hoped he wouldn't recognize me.

Why would he recognize you?

He went on, oblivious of the irony, as he claimed he and the students were neighbors. It was all over in five minutes, the room emptying as suddenly as it had filled. But as he turned to leave, the sun went behind a cloud and I was made visible. He saw me. The momentary surprise on his face, the eyebrows shooting upward as he stopped in midstride while his brain computed. His fusiform gyrus.

His what?

The hank of temporal lobe that recognizes faces.

You're saying the president knew who you were?

Why wouldn't he? We were roommates at Yale.

College roommates?

Well, yes, Yale's a college, Doc. Where I had taken a fall or two for him, as it happens. A week after his visit to my high school class has made the papers, I hear from the principal's office that a car will be waiting for me at the end of the school day. I can't say I was surprised. I'm driven to the White House, a marine saluting at the gate, and met at the door by a secretary who escorts me past the portraits of dead presidents into a meeting with one of the deputies to the chief of staff.

No president?

Something even worse. They want to appoint me director of the White House Office of Neurological Research. This will involve tracking neurological developments around the world and eventually putting together a commission of cognitive scientists to formulate brain research policy. The job comes with some modest G salary rating.

My goodness. All so sudden—

I had never heard of such an office and with good reason: It was newly devised and I would be the first appointee. You understand, I didn't have anything like a major reputation in cog science, so my first thought was that my old roomie was playing one of his practical jokes. [*thinking*] Because the government had to be deeply into neurological research and that had to have been ongoing for some time.

You think?

Come on, Doc, you have that look about you—

What look? All this is news to me.

—pretending not to know something you know all about. Don't you believe it's important for the government to predict how people will react to various stimuli, foreigners especially? Or to magnetically image the hallucinogenic mind? Or how to manipulate the brain's plasticity? Or a hundred other mental issues that can be useful to a government?

Brainwashing, you mean?

Brainwashing was the 1950s. I don't know why I talk to you. Anyway, it was a real enough offer and not a joke after all. They just wanted to keep an eye on me. I was to learn it was Peachums's idea.

Peachums?

That's what the president called him. The campaign manager. Said to be the president's brain. I wondered how much of that was left to be parceled out.

Peachums.

Or sometimes Plumsy—whatever was hairless.

I see.

As I was to realize, nobody, least of all the president, cared if I actually did what the job called for. The point was the next election. That some reporter would track me down, and I'd talk about our collegiate misadventures, of which there were quite a few. Like the incident of the bunsen burner. I had never spoken up about my famous roommate but did that mean I wouldn't? There I was, risen out of his dim past to become a staff concern. I had to sign a confidentiality statement: As an administration appointee I was subject to the law if I leaked information. I looked at the paper wondering whether to sign. It was a total clamp over my mouth.

But you accepted.

How could I ignore a presidential summons? [*thinking*] No, that's not the truth. It was as if he'd materialized, it was as if our life arcs—his so upward-reaching and mine looping into the depressed hemispheric depths—had described a perfect circle and there we were, superimposed in the same place at the same time. It felt inevitable.

I have to say I'm surprised you haven't mentioned any of this before now.

Why?

Well, it is unusual to say the least to find your old college roommate the president of the United States. Kind of story you can dine out on for a lifetime.

Are you suggesting I'm making this up?

No, of course not. I just wonder why you would wait this long before mentioning it?

I don't live vicariously, Doc. I didn't mention it before now I guess because I was talking about things more important to me.

OK.

Besides which he is nothing to brag about, is he? I didn't vote for him and wouldn't have voluntarily sought him out. He wouldn't have come up at all in these sessions except in the aftermath . . . the aftermath . . . [*thinking*] Name dropping is finally self-congratulatory, isn't it? But the fact that he was my roommate is nothing for which I've reason to congratulate myself. Maybe if I'd mentioned it at the beginning, like it wasn't the last thing in the world I wanted to talk about.

No, no, I believe you—you're here, aren't you?

I am politically informed, Doc. Apart from everything I've been telling you about myself, I am a citizen sensitive to his country's history. My roommate had gotten where he was by not quite the usual elected way. I knew how things had gone since—his chosen war, his anti-scientism. I knew all about him and the quality of the people around him. [*thinking*] Analyses had been done. All you had to do was read the newspaper. Those flights should never have happened. The intelligence was there.

You mean, you blame him?

Who am I to blame anyone for anything? But he was feckless, irresponsible, in over his head. . . . I believed he'd brought a fatal lassitude to the federal mind. On the theory that the president we get is the country we get. That was worth looking into, don't you think? I had long despaired of ever doing original work in my field. To start with the hypothesis that there is something like a government brain— I had the idea this was an opportunity of some kind.

Quite reasonable.

No, you don't understand. I kept a photo of Briony and our baby in my wallet. They are in the sun, in the park, Willa seated in Briony's arms as on a throne, and they are facing me, mother and child, two blondes, laughing, rising out of the picture to fill my eyes—

Yes?

So I signed the confidentiality agreement and became the head of the Office of Neurological Research in the White House basement. I meant to step into history, to act. To make a statement that would finally be the end of me.

What are you saying, Andrew?

And that's what I'd resolved the morning I stood on the corner with my coffee and paper waiting for the light to change.

VII

HELLO, DOC? I'm speaking to you from their old wall phone, the kind you crank up. Can you hear me?

Yes, Andrew, loud and clear.

No matter how old and broken-down things are, the life seems to work for them. It's uncanny. The local phone company must be as old as this house. And that flatbed truck, four on the floor, with the bald tires and the paint all weathered away—a kind of art object. So they walk to town. I do it myself. And the town too, shabby dimly lit little stores that have been there forever, but you find what you need. The hardware store—the guy who runs it, he does roofing, I kept picking up shingles in the yard so I engaged him to come patch thing up. There's a leak, all the old woman does is put a pail under it.

What about the screen door?

Oh, I fixed that. The mesh wasn't the problem, it was one of the hinges, the top hinge where it pulled away from the frame. But I took the whole thing down and did a job, new hinges, new mesh. Then of course the door frame is soft, spongy, so the real problem is termites. In due time, in due time. I've got my work cut out for me. Where the windows stick, where the floor squeaks. You don't know how good it is to concentrate on these things, the satisfaction of using your hands, figuring things out small-scale.

So you're planning to be there for a while. I was wondering where you were.

Something about this place. You know how some places stick in your mind for no reason? I mean, this is not a schloss in the mountains. It's not a finca under the palm trees. They've given me a room behind the kitchen with a mattress on the floor, and have otherwise ignored me. Totally incurious as to who I am, where I've come from. I can tell they don't look at me even when my back is turned. So I have every reason to feel safe here. No reason not to—I mean, I can't possibly bring harm to people with whom I have no relationship.

Do they ever thank you?

Listen, I'm calling to ask you something. She draws. I think I told you that.

What?

The kid, the little girl. She gets off the bus on the two-lane, comes running down the dirt road, flings her book bag on a kitchen chair, and sits down at the table with her colored pencils, her crayons, and her drawing pad, and she draws. It's all she wants to do. The old lady brings her a glass of milk and she's too busy drawing to drink it. Are you listening? Can you hear me?

Like we're in the same room.

When she senses that I'm looking at her through the screen door she scribbles over her drawings that she's worked on so carefully—puts the pencil in her fist and destroys what she's done.

So maybe you shouldn't watch her. Kids get shy about things that are meaningful to them. Do you say anything to her?

I've never said a thing. There's very little conversation in this farmhouse. Theirs is a relationship of mimes, the old woman and the kid. They seem to understand each other and what has to be done in any given moment— when to leave for school, when to go to bed—without talking about it. I've gotten to be just like them. I know when to come in for morning coffee, I know when to work on a project, I know when we have dinner, I know to nod good night. It's like a silent movie in this house.

You said you feel comfortable there.

Until now. Last night, after they had gone upstairs for the night, I went into the kitchen. They leave a light on. And I looked at the drawing she'd done that day on her pad of drawing paper. The kid. [*thinking*]

Andrew? You still there?

She draws well, far better than you'd think someone

of that age could draw. She's really good. It's all circus stuff. Acrobats, trapeze artists, tumblers, human pyramids. Girls in tutus standing on horses going around the ring. Little tiny figures all, perfectly formed.

Andrew?

They're coming. I'm hanging up now.

VIII

ALL RIGHT, if my life as an undergraduate is what interests you: I never expected to have him as a roommate. His family name, after all. And I, the financial aid student. But the college forbade preferential treatment—every freshman was no more than that. He laughed at my clumsiness. We would be in frequent trouble, a pair of misfits. [*thinking*] I guess it was just a matter of time and here we were again.

What was the incident of the bunsen burner you mentioned?

Our digs were a center of social life. People gathered around. It was mostly him, of course, but I too became known on campus—a second banana, as it were. I must have realized at some point that I had no identity without him. Because he was who he was, I was who I was. I did manage to keep up with my studies, which drove him mad. I'd be at my desk cramming for an exam and he couldn't bear that, he'd drag me off to a bar. I'll say this in his favor, hanging out with him I got braver with girls and by my junior year I was in a fairly serious relationship. But around him, the pressure was to be a clown, to find a way to make him laugh. Not just me but other guys too, that desire to fulfill his expectations. And every once in a while, after a few beers, what came to the fore was his mean streak, because he did have one. [*thinking*] His fooling around could segue into hurting people. Or humiliating them. His grades were dismal, he never cracked a book. It wasn't as if he couldn't have done better by applying himself. He was a contrarian. He was making a stand.

And so what was that incident of the bunsen burner?

In the inorganic chem lab. I was standing right where it happened with a shard of beaker sticking in my cheek and blood running down my chin. Something had exploded, I didn't know what, but the room was filled with smoke, people were coughing, shouting, the sprinkler system had turned on, in one instant the lab was a total disaster. It was funny, actually. The professor, running in and waving away the smoke, assumed I was the culprit. I didn't argue.

Well, this doesn't sound like something they would feel endangered by in an election thirty years later.

Well, it wasn't the only thing. I tutored him on occasion.

So?

Onsite, as it were. Where we were taking the exam.

I see.

Yes. But why would I reveal something now that would make me look just as bad? Given an academic career to uphold. Such as it is.

I understand.

The incident of the bunsen burner got me a semester of probation. And an invitation to go home with him on the spring break.

A cold glance from the formidable mother, a limp distracted handshake from the father. That's what I remember. Their son seemed to accept their rude offhand greetings as typical. I stood there with my backpack while staff ran by in some urgency. The household was busy preparing for dinner guests. I can tell you my roommate and I smoked dope in the upstairs of a huge floor-length duplex and not a book in sight.

Andrew looked out the window—one of those unopenable bronze-framed windows, and all he could see was a building across the wide empty street that was just like the one in which he stood looking out at what he thought might be a shadowed reflection of himself. These were condominiums designed to look like office buildings, architectural statements celebrating the prevailing culture. He'd never seen a city like this, spread out on a flat plane. It baked in heat that shimmered up in the afternoon, and with its endless parking lots all filled under a hot sky and, in the downtown center, these characterless skyscrapers covered in dark glass. Andrew believed it could not be called a city if it did not have narrow streets filled with people and shops, horns blowing, the sidewalks overflowing and a nightlife into the early hours. Here everything went still after sundown, the traffic lights mindlessly directing nonexistent traffic. The two college boys were invited to the dinner that first evening and seated down at the far end of an enormous table that stood under three glistening chandeliers. Even I could tell the place settings were of the finest china, with heavy silver, and thin-stemmed wineglasses that contained the light as small golden suns. And this was just their pied-à-terre. We sat below the salt along with the secretaries and family business flunkies, none of whom were interested in talking, a spiritless lot suffering their lesser stature in silence while the formal reception and many toasts went on at the far end. It was a colorful dinner, in fact, all these sheiks and princes in their keffiyehs and designer floor-length tunics, men without women, mustached, bearded, stately, impressive, and in fact dressed appropriately in cotton for this desert. But when it came to a close and everyone stood and moved en masse out of the dining room, this is what I want to tell you: Andrew accidentally stepped on the train—if that was what it was—of one of the princes. It ripped, a flap of it fell open, and there in front of me was this hairy leg. It wore a running shoe. The things we remember. A moment later my roomie pulled me into a side door, running me up some back stairs two at a time till we got to his rooms and fell on our beds laughing.

The next morning I was told to leave by one of the secretaries. The heir apparent excused the chauffeur and ruefully drove me to the airport. The airport had the family name and there were huge photographs of his mother and father above the escalators. I'll see you back there, he said, uncharacteristically gloomy. And Andrew understood that for a moment he'd been brought into the family dynamic as an incidental player in his roommate's ongoing struggle.

IX

S O THERE YOU HAVE some of my memory, in case you doubted me.

I didn't doubt you.

I was surprised to find him a middle-aged man. Unless you've seen someone on a daily basis, in which case the changes are imperceptible, it takes a moment before the remembered image dissolves.

Hadn't you seen photographs, interviews on television, speeches?

Not the same as running into a life up close. Later, when I was sitting around in the Oval Office, I recognized the same twist of the mouth before the punch line of some dumb joke. That was the same. And the cockiness was there. But the eyes, a little bit scared, the eyes. Like he'd realized what he'd become. The hair gunmetal dull, some thinning on the crown.

As for the others, Chaingang and Rumbum, they were small men, I mean physically small, the one red of face, scowling of mouth, the other impeccably tailored and barbered, the instincts of a peacock, but both smaller in scale than their pictures, so that was interesting.

Who did you say?

It was a game of his—subtle, really—a sign of his affection, a kind of honorific, or maybe a brand such as you burn into a steer, because it was also a means of letting you know he owned you, knew what you were in essence. Like with Peachums. So the two key men in his administration, the ones who ran things, were Chaingang and Rumbum.

And what were you?

He stamped me as well, with his breakout smile. I was Android.

I see.

Uncanny, as if some dendrite winding through his brain was snappier than the billions of others. Because I was Android, all right. Tap me with your knuckle, hear the clunk.

So there you were.

He would never ask Android anything about himself, personal stuff, how his life had gone, whether he was married, those questions you ask if you have any curiosity. It was as if we were still at Yale.

Well, they had probably done a background check.

Why would he bother reading it?

Anyway, there you were.

Yes, to people's puzzlement. Because I had to be a game first of all. Bright and early the first day I was there he summoned me to the Oval Office.

Just sit over here, Android, and don't say a word. Don't look up, don't pay any attention. Here, read this magazine. Make believe you're at the dentist's office. And so I sat there off to the side while he conducted the morning's business, receiving staff, holding meetings, my presence unexplained. As if he didn't know I was there, as if I was an illusion of the others. Maybe I was Secret Service, though I hardly looked the part. But, if he didn't seem to notice me, nobody could say anything. What a good time he was having keeping a straight face.

And were you enjoying the joke?

Would you in my position? The joke was my ano-nymity. I was like a shadow he'd cast. As if I was still his roommate. After a day or two of this, like everything in Washington it turned into news. That the president had a stranger hanging around his office was reported in the *Spectator*, a four-page subscription weekly: MYSTERY MAN IN THE WHITE HOUSE! That makes two of us, the president said.

Chaingang scripted the White House response for the administration spokesman. Of course no reporter would be allowed near me. It was put out that I was a dear college chum just visiting for a few days. That had an ele-ment of truth but didn't go down with the bloggers. I was to the president as Clyde Tolson was to J. Edgar

Hoover. Or the president was seriously ill and required a physician constantly by his side. This was not to be borne: The chief of staff said I had to go. My presence was damaging to the president's image as the leader of the free world. And there were questions of national security. Not that I ever heard anything interesting—they all talked like the newspapers. But I was remanded to my basement office in the cleaning closet. If the president wanted to kick back, he snuck down there when no one was looking.

What about your White House Office of Neurological Research? Why wasn't that mentioned?

That the president's science advisor knew nothing about? Never mind the CIA and the NSA. It would have sent the memos flying. Resignations. I might have actually had to do the work I was supposed to do. No, that was a secret that couldn't be leaked. You remember the point was to make sure I kept my mouth shut.

Peachums's idea.

Yes. Like the others, he didn't like to see me upstairs. I heard him shouting one morning. As I walked into the Oval Office, he stormed out, taking up most of the doorway. But my old buddy would want me to have coffee just to sit around and talk about anything except being president. His war was not going well. He'd invaded the wrong country. You can't imagine the anxiety that produces.

Amazing.

What's amazing? You think I'm making this up?

No, it's just that—

I was a story for a day or two before it all suddenly and mysteriously disappeared. Where were you at the time? You of all people. And if not, it's in the file, it would have to be.

What file?

Come on, Doc, at least have some respect. Do you know what Mind Reading is in cog science talk? It's not about some magician up on a stage working his audience.

No?

No. Mind Reading is what, at the right temporoparietal junction of the brain, allows us in our social lives to know deductively, instinctively, what other people are thinking. The mood they're in—happiness, boredom, whatever. Mind reading is our way of characterizing human sensitivity, like knowing, for instance, when someone is pretending not to know something.

I'm sorry you feel that way.

The *Post* and the *Times* had got as far as my past life—two marriages, one death, one divorce, a child farmed out, another died in infancy. I came to appreciate investigative reporting. It's like obituary writing—they get everything but the feeling. They had my college grade average—3.25, something like an exoneration in my mind. And an old photograph from the college newspaper, the roomies with big smiles on their faces and arms around each other's shoulders right there on the front page of the *Post*. I realized for the first time that, apart from my curly hair, we were look-alikes. There was almost a familial resemblance, at least then. I had since worn not as well as he. Surely you know something of this. Or else why am I here?

Good morning, class. Good morning, red of face and scowl of mouth. Good morning, starched of shirt and waved of hair. This morning we will speak of consciousness. Where does it come from? What does it do with itself? Does it connive? Does it seek advantages? How does it learn its ways—as billions of neurons self-conceiving in neural circuits, revise, adjust, reorganize, multiply responding behaviorally to outer-world creature experience—in a process of natural selection or neural Darwinism, according to Edelman? Does that include you, pretty-boy warmaker? Are you the culmination of this evolutionary brainwork? Crick, on the other hand, opts for the role of the claustrum or maybe the thalamus. Abjure claustrumphobia. Remember the thalamus! In any event you have no soul. But neither do Edelman or

Crick. And neither does scowler here, though he will kill
to prove that he has one. But that is the pretense of the
brain. We have to be wary of our brains. They make our
decisions before we make them. They lead us to still wa-
ters. They renounceth free will. And it gets weirder: If
you slice a brain down the middle, the left hemisphere
and the right hemisphere will operate self-sufficiently
and not know what the other is doing. But don't think
about these things, because it won't be you anyway doing
the thinking. Just follow your star. Live in the presumptions of the socially constructed life. Abhor science. Sort
of believe in God. Put your failings behind you. Present
your self-justifications to the bathroom mirror.

You really disliked those men, didn't you.

Chaingang and Rumhum were self-appointed world
strategists. They had ranks of ideologues and think-tank
warriors behind them. The president was only that.
These were complicated relationships among the three
men, and at moments he had to feel outnumbered and
outclassed. For every instance that he went along with
their bidding, however persuasive and in accord with his
own instincts, there had to be some resentment there,
don't you think? I understood that he was using me as a
prod to annoy them, having me test them, knowing it

was an affront to make them hear me lecture on neurological developments around the world. That's what he
kept saying: Android (with a sly smile), let's hear about
the neurological developments around the world.

Well, Mr. President, in Switzerland they are building
a megacomputer to emulate the human brain. Slowly but
surely they're building circuitry to mimic its synaptical,
neuronal capacities. As complex as our brains are, the
number of elements that make them work are finite.
That means it's just a matter of time before we have a
working out-of-body brain.

Is that true?

That's what Chaingang asked with an ironic smile.
This is not an old science fiction movie you're giving us?
The president had his hands full with Chaingang and
Rumbum, men he'd appointed who had more or less
taken over where the important decisions were to be
made. So his next joke was to announce that I was a
brain researcher doing a study of executive brains like
theirs. They were busy men, they had things to do, a war
to run, and here he was having fun at their expense.

Your brains are looking good, he told them. Like a
promising field for oil drilling.

They were not loath to show their irritation. In their
eyes the president was a kind of dauphin who they felt
lacked gravitas, to say nothing of a reasonable attention

span. Their belief in their intellectual superiority was at odds with the fact that he was of the historically elected and they were not. He could affect a presidential strut walking to his helicopter, but he was not the real kingly thing as they felt they would be were they in his shoes. [*thinking*] In other countries it was men like these who mounted coups.

You saw all that?

When you're in a room with the president of the United States you become very observant. My presence enraged the two men. So much so that I thought I would go along with the president and run a thought experiment. They believed I was putting them under the microscope, so why not? When in the history of the United States had a private citizen ever had a chance like this? But it had to be quick. It could work only until the president lost interest. That didn't give me much time.

Chaingang and Rumbum had made their careers in government. Their minds were wired into well-established neuronal circuits that found expression in the vocabularies of war, detention, physical torture, political power, social gossip, sex, and money. So I cleared my throat and gave them each a pad and a pencil, and explained the cog sci prisoners' dilemma game to them. Of course I didn't send them out of the room as I had the high schoolers, I just told them each, privately, outside of the hearing of the other, to imagine that the president knew of their conspiracy to overthrow the government because his co-conspirator had betrayed him. He could say nothing or he could betray his colleague in turn. Their decisions would have greater or lesser punitive consequences in the hands of the attorney general. They were to write down the decision to betray or not to betray their co-conspirator.

They put up with this?

Like children given a task. They sat at opposite ends of one of the Oval Office sofas, their backs turned as they bent over their pads—with frowns, a closing of eyes here, a rubbing of forehead there—in the performance of heavy thought. I had warned them not to look at each other, but that was unnecessary. This was game theory, after all. Betray your co-conspirator and you're in trouble, for you've admitted your guilt, but if you don't betray him and he betrays you, he goes free and you're headed for the slammer big-time. Only if neither of you betrays the other is the case against you dropped.

And what happened?

These men had served in various capacities over several administrations. Now they were at the very top. How had they gotten there? Who more than they knew how politics worked? So of course each of them, figuring the best possible outcome for himself, had no choice but to betray.

How the president laughed when I handed him the pads on which they'd written their decisions. A no-brainer, he said.

You made yourself known there, didn't you.

I had no illusions, though. He needed a sidekick, a familiar, but for how long? He gave me one of those little lapel flags they liked to wear, so you knew they were patriots.

Yes?

Pinned it on me as you would a medal. I was now one of the good guys. Though as it turned out, my job as the director of the phantom White House Office of Neurological Research lasted not quite three weeks.

But a lifetime, as it were.

Yes. One afternoon, before I left for the day, the president showed me the Lincoln Bedroom on the second floor. Lincoln never slept there, of course, it wasn't even a bedroom when he lived there. What was it, a study? But anyway the heavy Victorian furniture and swooping draperies looked as if Lincoln might have slept there. I said hello to the tenants—

The tenants?

Well, you know, this is where the president put up big-time donors for an overnight thrill. A calm enough couple they were, not at all overwhelmed to be in the president's company, the man some decades grayer than the woman. They were in the act of unpacking. When you look at money it doesn't seem anything but human. We all huddled over the desk where a copy of the Gettysburg Address was under glass.

So you were getting around in the White House.

I noticed of the young wife that she was tall with a good figure, but the face was as if ceramicized, somehow, the eyes glancing at me without seeming to realize I was there. A golden fall of hair as shiny and stiff as if shellacked. If Briony had been with me she would have felt cowed, my poor innocent, but just for a moment. This was an entire aspect of American life she knew nothing about. On the other hand, looking at Briony's simple face-washed beauty, and the pure being that shone from her blue eyes, this woman would have felt her heart sinking for having spent her life affecting a sophistication she did not feel.

You knew all this from looking at her?

Thoughts of Briony gave me all sorts of perceptive advantages. It was as if something of her mind was still alive in me.

Is that cognitive science?

Not really. It's more like suffering.

X

H E DID KEEP a neat desk, the president, a few papers aligned under a little snow globe that served as a paperweight. You shook the globe and the snow drifted over a child sledding down a hillside. I had begun to feel sorry for my old roommate. He lived with his ineptitude. From my basement window I could see a more or less constant procession of limos driving up: generals and admirals, diplomats, cabinet members, visiting foreign dignitaries, all of whom he had to see because he was said to be the leader of the free world. He seemed more relaxed in those arts awards evenings where performers sang and medals were given out to film directors, playwrights, and actors. I was invited to one of those and sat in the rear where no one noticed me.

I had begun to savor my role there in the White House, having accepted a lieutenancy in the little war between the president and his closest advisors. It was as if right there in the Oval Office the prevailing contentiousness of the world outside had to be honored. It was as if the wars they were conducting were to be symbolized in their own relationships. I thought how contention makes us human. How every form of it is practiced religiously, from gentlemanly debate to rape and pillage, from dirty political attacks to assassinations. Our nighttime street fights outside of bars, our slapping arguments in plush bedrooms, our murderous mutterings in the divorce courts. We had parents who beat their children, schoolyard bullies, career-climbing killers in ties and suits, drivers cutting one another off, people pushing one another through the subway doors, nations making war, dropping bombs, swarming onto beaches, the daily military coups, the endless disappearances, the dispossessed dying in their tent camps, the ethnic cleansing crusades, drug wars, terrorist murders, and all violence in every form countenanced somewhere by some religion or other . . . and for its entertainment politicidal, genocidal, suicidal humanity attending its beloved kick-boxing matches, and cockfights, or losing its paychecks on the blackjack felt and then going back to work undercutting the competition, scamming, ponzi-ing, poisoning . . . and the impassioned lovers of their times contending in their own little universe of sex, one turgidly wanting it, the other wincingly refusing it.

Have you left anything out?

So I had been brought here, I thought, to give my old roommate some measure of satisfaction in his peculiar struggle with Chaingang and Rumbum. But there was a country to be run and they were the president's two closest advisors, and after all he needed them just as they needed him. So after a few more of Android's reports of neurological developments around the world, I detected a shift in the dynamic: I'd been there for a couple of weeks. At a certain moment one day they all had the same look on their faces, an effort not to laugh, and I understood that a new alliance in the great diplomatic tradition had been effected. I was alone versus the triumvirate and the joke was on me—the three of them in collusion to put me in a foolscap with bells—and all this while the world waited for the next civil war, the next tanking of the market, the next suicide bombing, the next tsunami, the next earthquake, the next leakage of radioactive material from the next defective nuclear plant—this game of seeing how long Android would go on with the show before he realized that he was their cruel sport, that they were taking a break, the three of them, right there in the White House—and I, the fool, was bringing a bit of comedy to their dark, contentious, power-charged, world-ruling day.

So there came that moment of realization and it was time to let them know who they were dealing with. I gave them Android's last lecture on neurological developments around the world. I told them the great problem confronting neuroscience is how the brain becomes the mind. How that three-pound knitting ball makes you feel like a human being. I said we were working on it, and if they valued their lives, or life as they knew it, they would do well to divert whatever government funding there was for neuroscience and add it to the defense budget. More rockets, landmines, jet fighters—all those things you love, I said. Because if we figure out how the brain gives us consciousness, we will have learned how to replicate consciousness. You understand that, don't you, Doc?

I do.

So what, you mean computers who talk back?, Chain-gang said. I've seen that in the movies. Computers, of course, I said, and animals genetically developed to have more than the primary consciousness of animals. To have feelings, states of mind, memory, longing. He means like in Disney, Rumbum said, and they laughed. I laughed as well. Yes, I said, and with all of that the end of the mythic human world we've had since the Bronze Age. The end of our dominion. The end of the Bible and all the stories we've told ourselves until now.

Andrew, you really think that?

How insulated these men were. They were imperial in their selfhood, these corporate culturists running a government. They lived, heedless, infallible. They understood contention and expected nothing else. I told them it depressed me to be in the same room with them. The president looked at me—did I mean him as well? You all live unquestioningly inside the social reality—war, God, money—that other people invented long ago, I said, and you take these things for raw existence. It was quite a speech I gave them.

Apparently.

They were careless of life, I said, they were prime examples of human insufficiency, I said, and I told them I spoke as an authority on the subject. Then I took a deep breath and did a handstand.

A what?

It just came over me, I was up on my hands almost before I realized it. Perhaps it was the image of Briony on the high bar—my first glimpse of her—that animated me, my brain having decided that this was the thing to do, a mimetic act to bring her into resolution there in the White House. At least that is my interpretation now. At the time it was possibly no more than an act of inspired madness. Or maybe it was just my brain saying if it's a fool they want it's a fool they will get. Or maybe I just wanted to be out of there.

So you actually did that?

What I'm saying. I'd never done a bona fide handstand before. I was another man in the Oval Office.

I can tell you that as Andrew wavered there, his arms aching, his feet moving to and fro like the shuttles of a loom, he found himself weeping, either from the effort or from the image in his mind, Briony smiling, her clear blue eyes in their sturdy innocence assessing him. What was she saying? I heard her voice, her soundless voice: Going for a run, Andrew. For her morning snack, Willa likes the applesauce.

And the door closes and then the arc of her balletic leap into the fire.

I think I groaned, the blood pounding in my head, but it seemed to me a matter of honor to remain upside down as long as possible. They, the president and Chaingang and Rumbum, had risen from their chairs, Chaingang stepping behind the president's desk and shouting into a phone. I collapsed then, landing not the way you're supposed to, but painfully, with a thud, and I think now that almost simultaneously a pair of marines in dress uniform were yanking me to my feet and twisting my arms behind my back. So one way or another it was a very physical day for me.

Apparently it was.

What did you say?

I was agreeing.

But it was more than that. I doubt if anyone had ever done a handstand in the Oval Office before. Really it was a triumph. I had for a moment risen out of my characteristic humility, my ordinary citizenness, and in one upside-down gesture achieved equity with these governors of my country. I knew the future whereas they didn't. You might not have known from all I've spoken of my life that I was not without a keen political awareness. As I stood there, functionally disabled by the two marines, Chaingang and Rumbum were deciding what would be my fate. They ordered my arrest. Rumbum saying I had threatened the life of the president. Get this fool out of here, he said.

Make that a Holy Fool, I said.

Is that what you felt you were?

What else could I be if my old roommate was The Pretender? Because that's what he unquestionably was. And never again would I be another man according to the situation. I could feel my brain becoming me—we were resolved as one. As I was led to the door, I turned and said what a Holy Fool would say: You are only the worst so far, there is far worse to come. Perhaps not tomorrow. Perhaps not next year, but you have shown us the path into the Dark Wood. I suppose that was Dante I was doing right there. My roommate didn't like to hear it. Oh, come on, Android, he called, lighten up. Was he asking me to retract? Was he expecting my blessing? But how could I? What makes a fool holy is that he mourns for his country.

I stood tall, nodded to my guards, and they led me away.

XI

S o, Doc, how long have I been here?

It's been a while.

And you won't tell me where this is?

I can't.

It's not home.

How do you know that?

The air. There's a softness to it. It gives one a settled sweet earth taste of the spring air. I've never experienced that in the New World. I think this is a countryside of low hills and wildflowers and grape arbors. I can't see over the walls, but in the exercise yard I hear birds and they're not the birds of home. Also it stays light long into the evening. I think this is Mediterranean Europe you people have dropped me into, and it's not bad—the torture is not exquisite but only in my reflection of what has happened to me—apart from talking to you I have no one and no lawyer has been appointed and I'm being held without trial and it's already been indefinitely. That's celestial time, you know. I'm sentenced to roll round with the planet, to count the suns, the moons, the seasons. . . . Do you think I threatened the life of the president?

No, actually.

Yet I won't accuse you of following orders and being a nullity. You know why?

Why?

Without you to talk to I'd be even worse off than I am.

You don't have to worry.

Although I have my collected MT on the shelf I think how can I keep my mind from going? And if my mind goes can the country be far behind?

So you're saying there's a connection?

My mind is shot through with visions, dreams, and the actions and words of people I don't know. I hear soundless voices, phantoms loom up out of my sleep and onto the wall, lingering there, cringing in anguish, curling up in visible contortions of pain and crying out wordlessly for my help. What are you doing to me!, I shout, and fall back into bed only to stare at the black ceiling and my room is a darkened movie theater where another silent horror show is about to begin. I speak of a broached integrity. Only by hoping that there is a science behind this am I able to endure it. Perhaps I'm carrying in my brain matter the neuronal record of previous ages. I know you haven't gone through anything like this, you're too accepting of your own experiences. They thrive in you, maxing out to your brain's capacity. But when you're as unfeeling as I am—

Ah, we're back to that?

—there may be an opportunity for the dormant genetic microtraces from earlier times to express themselves in dreams.

So is this cognitive science?

Not quite yet. It's still only suffering.

Tell me, Doc, am I a computer?

What?

Am I the first computer invested with consciousness? With terrible dreams, with feelings, with grief, with longing?

No, Andrew, you're a human being.

Well, you would say that.

I see you've let your beard grow, your hair. You could indeed be the Holy Fool. But it needs something.

What's this?

A Yankees baseball cap. Your wardrobe needed refreshing.

How old is Willa now?

Twelve.

And where are they all living?

We've been through this—

Where?

They're in New Rochelle.

In their old house?

Yes.

Martha and Martha's large husband.

Yes.

And they need my agreement? Why? A judge will rule in their favor—Martha has raised her since she was a baby. And I'm an enemy combatant.

You're not an enemy combatant.

Whatever I am I haven't much legal standing, have I?

It's for the child's sake. Here are the papers.

So my daughter will have Boris Godunov, that drunk, that Pretender, for a legal father.

He's in AA. Doesn't drink anymore.

When did they get back together, the loving couple?

A few years ago, I think. Three or four.

And where did she take my child when she disappeared?

As I've told you, Martha settled in a small town in western Pennsylvania. A farm inherited from an aunt and uncle.

Do they have the finances to keep my daughter as she deserves?

They are not without resources. She teaches piano

again and he has a master class in voice. They are both at Juilliard.

It says here Willa is not to be told about me. It says I may never approach her, reveal myself to her as her father—

She has no reason to believe that Martha is not her mother. I'm not sure how the status of the husband will be represented in her eyes.

—or that her real mother died trying to save people.

Is that what you think now?

Yes.

I don't imagine they would tell the child that.

Well, then, the hell with them!

Oh, for God's sake, why can't you be reasonable for a change? Think of someone besides yourself.

Oh, Doc. I do. I think all the time of my two girls. I want to read to them like MT did to his little girls, making up stories to help them get to sleep. He says, "They think my tales are better than paregoric, and quicker."

Andrew, please—

He wrote down this one story for other fathers to use? Every name, and where possible every word, will have a cat in it—Catasauqua, Cataline, cattalactic. And the girls keep interrupting. What is a catadrome, Papa? I'll look, he says, pretending to consult the dictionary. Ah, it is a racecourse. I thought it was a tenpin alley, but cats do not play tenpins when they are feeling well, but they do run races. Thank you, Papa, the little girl says. Yes, he says, and the story continues.

Andrew—

MT's invented silliness at his children's bedtime. How he is their protector, and the world's a safe snug place at their bedtime. How when they are grown they will remember this tale and laugh with love for their father. How this is his redemption.

ABOUT THE AUTHOR

E. L. DOCTOROW's works of fiction include *Homer & Langley, The March, Billy Bathgate, Ragtime, The Book of Daniel, City of God, Welcome to Hard Times, Loon Lake, World's Fair, The Waterworks,* and *All the Time in the World.* Among his honors are the National Book Award, three National Book Critics Circle awards, two PEN/Faulkner awards, and the presidentially conferred National Humanities Medal. In 2009 he was short-listed for the Man Booker International Prize, honoring a writer's lifetime achievement in fiction, and in 2012 he won the PEN/Saul Bellow Award for Achievement in American Fiction, given to an author whose "scale of achievement over a sustained career places him in the highest rank of American literature." In 2013 the American Academy of Arts and Letters awarded him the Gold Medal for Fiction.